"You scared, Blaine?"

She faked a pout, sticking her lip out as she teased him. "Of little old me?"

He rolled his eyes, but his smile was evident as he joined her on the blanket. "You're too much, Eden."

"So, we're basically alone now." *Or at least as close to alone as we're gonna get without me crawling into your lap.* She watched him, taking in his moon-dappled handsomeness. The dim lighting seemed to enhance his features, especially the golden flecks in his dark eyes. He was a temptation in the flesh; her body craved him even though her mind knew better than to get lost in him again. The question was, how much longer would she be able to lead with logic? "What do you want to talk about?"

He cleared his throat. "If I'm being honest..."

"Please do," she encouraged.

"I want to talk about kissing you again."

* * *

After Hours Redemption by Kianna Alexander is part of the 404 Sound series.

Dear Reader,

Thank you for picking up a copy of *After Hours Redemption*. My purpose in writing this story, and the larger series, is to share my love of hip-hop with you. It was the soundtrack to my formative years and will always hold a place in my heart. What better way to share the love than with a steamy romance? Blaine and Eden's story will take you into the glamorous fast-paced world of the Atlanta music scene, where dreams of stardom can become reality. What a backdrop to fall in love against, huh?

Happy reading!

Kianna

KIANNA ALEXANDER

—

AFTER HOURS REDEMPTION

HARLEQUIN
DESIRE

My humblest thanks to my writing buddy Kaia for the intel and the
encouragement. I'd also like to thank my Destin Divas, who are a
constant source of inspiration and always give me the extra push
when I need it. Thanks to the readers who continually support my
work—I truly appreciate y'all. And thanks to the producers, the
songwriters, the artists, the sound engineers—all those people
who make it possible for us all to enjoy so much great music.

HARLEQUIN®
DESIRE™

Recycling programs
for this product may
not exist in your area.

ISBN-13: 978-1-335-20942-9

After Hours Redemption

Copyright © 2020 by Eboni Manning

Harlequin Enterprises ULC
22 Adelaide St. West, 40th Floor
Toronto, Ontario M5H 4E3, Canada
www.Harlequin.com

Printed in U.S.A.

Kianna Alexander, like any good Southern belle, wears many hats: loving wife, doting mama, advice-dispensing sister and gabbing girlfriend. She's a voracious reader, an amateur seamstress and occasional painter in oils. Chocolate, American history, sweet tea and Idris Elba are a few of her favorite things. A native of the Tar Heel state, Kianna still lives there with her husband, two kids and a collection of well-loved vintage '80s Barbie dolls. You can keep up with Kianna's releases and appearances by signing up for her mailing list at www.authorkiannaalexander.com/sign-up.

Books by Kianna Alexander

Harlequin Desire

404 Sound

After Hours Redemption

Harlequin Kimani Romance

This Tender Melody
Every Beat of My Heart
A Sultry Love Song
Tempo of Love

Visit her Author Profile page at Harlequin.com, or www.authorkiannaalexander.com, for more titles.

You can also find Kianna Alexander on Facebook, along with other Harlequin Desire authors, at www.Facebook.com/harlequindesireauthors!

For Tameya. It was written in the stars.

One

First, I didn't get a contract. Now I'm stuck driving home in a monsoon.

Peering through the water streaming down the windshield, Eden Voss kept an eye out for the turn going into her southwest Atlanta neighborhood. Typical of any Tuesday night, city traffic had been akin to driving in a demolition derby, and the rain only exacerbated that. The farther she got away from the city proper, the more she relaxed. She'd just spent three hours sitting in a smoky hookah lounge in Midtown with a producer and his newest act, discussing whether her songwriting might be a good fit for them. If the young artist had been as decisive as he'd been flirtatious, the meeting might have actually led to something concrete.

She wondered what she would have been like if her

dreams of singing stardom had come true. Those ambitions were long ago laid to rest. However, she knew that if she had made it, she wouldn't have been so disrespectful as to ogle another industry professional, especially during what was supposed to be a business meeting.

Eden pushed those thoughts away, concentrating instead on making it home intact. Even with the wipers going full blast, visibility was limited at best. Carefully navigating the streets of her subdivision, she turned into her driveway just as another bright flash of lightning illuminated the sky. She shook her head, grateful she'd bought a house with a garage. After she'd pulled inside it and closed the shutter on the storm raging outside, she wrinkled her nose at the lingering smoke clinging to her clothes.

Moments later, she unlocked the side door and entered the house through the kitchen. She could see the glow of the television as she approached the living room. A smile curved her lips. *She waited up for me... again.* Her older cousin and roommate had a protective streak that still lingered from when they were kids.

She kicked off her shoes and padded into the room. "Ainsley, you didn't have to wait up."

Her cousin was stretched out on the couch, tucked beneath her favorite oversize throw emblazoned with the cover of OutKast's classic album *ATLiens*. "I know, I know. But I was already watching a *Law & Order* marathon."

She chuckled, seeing the familiar program on the TV. "Okay, Mom. Coop's upstairs asleep?"

Ainsley nodded. "You know my son. He treasures his

sleep above all else." At ten years old, sleep and *Mine-craft* were Cooper's two favorite pastimes. She shifted around a bit until she sat up. "How did the meeting go?"

Thinking back on the meeting made her cringe. "Girl, I don't even know. The producer seemed into it, but I think the singer paid more attention to my boobs than my pitch."

"Oh, what a creep. Is this a singer I know?"

"Levi Duncan. Newer artist, supposedly the second coming of Usher."

Ainsley's brow cocked. "Second coming? Please. Usher's had like ten 'second comings,' plus he's still around. These R & B dudes now are a dime a dozen. Very few stand out."

"You're right about that. Have you ever heard of him?"

"Nah." Ainsley shook her head. "Sounds like a real character. If that's how he acts, he'll fit right in with the rest of the jerks in the music industry."

She felt her lips stretch into a thin line as the memories of those days rose within. Late nights in the studio, poring over the lyric sheets with Blaine Woodson. The man who'd crushed all her hopes and dreams. She could still smell his woodsy cologne. Handsome, talented...and duplicitous. He'd brought her into the music business, along with Ainsley and their friend Cambria. He'd praised their talents, filled their heads with fantasies of what could be.

She'd fallen for his words, and in the process, fallen in love. But when the time came for him to really show he believed in her, he'd disappointed her in the worst way.

"Scoot over." Eden flopped down on the sofa next to her cousin. "Anything interesting happen at the studio today?"

"I heard one of the newer artists in the booth today, laying down backing vocals. Brought back memories, ya know?"

Eden laughed. "I bet." She leaned in close, even though there was no one else in the room, her tone conspiratorial. "I heard a rumor that T.I. was coming by. Did he?"

Looking amused, she shook her head. "No. Somebody from his label was there, but no action in the booth just yet."

"Well, keep me posted. When he's there, I might just have to drop by and bring you lunch."

Ainsley laughed. "You're a mess. But I'll let you know if I spot the Rubber Band Man."

She fist-bumped her. "My homegirl."

A brilliant flash illuminated the room, followed by a loud crack of thunder reverberating through the house.

Ainsley cast a wary eye toward the window. "It's a mess out there."

A memory popped into her mind then, and she asked, "Remember how Mom and Aunt Mimi would call it 'good sleeping weather'?"

"I remember." Ainsley's expression took on a wistful tone. "I miss them."

She squeezed her cousin's shoulder. "Me, too." It had been three years since the bus accident had claimed the lives of their mothers, who'd been traveling together for a church trip. Eden felt the tug in her chest, the same tug she felt whenever she thought of how much she missed her mother and her favorite aunt. Their deaths had forged an even closer bond between her and Ainsley. Eden yawned. "I'm beat, Ains. I'm going up to bed."

"I'll be up after this episode."

She extricated herself from the soft cushions and headed toward the foyer.

More lightning flashed, and before she could reach the staircase, another wall-rattling boom of thunder swept through the house.

This time, a huge, splintering crash followed.

Eden's head jerked toward the upper floor of the house, where it seemed the sound had come from.

What the hell was that?

"Mom!" Cooper screamed from his upstairs bedroom in the far corner of the house. "Help!"

Oh no.

Ainsley jumped up from the couch, and she and Eden raced up the stairs, their hearts pounding.

"We're excited to welcome your newest artist, Blaine."

The voice of Rupert Wright, A&R director for Hamilton House Records, broke through Blaine Woodson's thoughts. *Damn. I should've had that second cup of coffee.* It was just before ten Wednesday morning, and he had some serious midweek doldrums going on. Straightening in his stiff-backed chair at the conference table, he smiled. "I'm glad to hear that, Rupert. I think it's going to be an amazing partnership."

"Wonderful." Rupert redirected his attention. "And Miss Brown, let me be the first to welcome you to the Hamilton House family."

"Thanks. And you can call me Naiya." Twenty-three-year-old singer Naiya B. sat next to Blaine in a matching chair. Her gaze shifted around the room as if she were studying the wall displays. "I see you've got quite a few plaques under your belt."

Blaine gave Naiya's shoulder a quick pat. "And soon your platinum plaque will be up there with the rest." Her viral videos, featuring her singing covers of classic songs by the likes of Phyllis, Whitney and Toni, had first attracted Blaine's attention two months ago. She possessed a stunning vocal talent. He'd reached out to her, and she'd signed to his boutique label, Against the Grain Records. His subsidiary status under AMGI/Hamilton House provided most of his operating budget.

Naiya's warm smile conveyed her delight. "I'm really excited about all this. I have so much I want to say, and I appreciate this chance to express myself."

Seeing that sparkle in her eyes, Blaine couldn't help smiling. She reminded him of someone else. A curly-haired young woman with cocoa eyes lit up like the Vegas Strip. Sharp, witty, beautiful and wildly talented. *Eden Voss.* She'd been a part of the very first group signed to his label, and he'd shared a unique connection with her. But their chemistry extended far beyond music. He'd let her go in order to grow his label. It had been less than ideal, but Hamilton House held the purse strings, and he'd had to follow their edicts.

Rupert's bushy gray brows furrowed slightly. "What's your vision for your first album, Naiya?"

She brightened and gave a brief account of her plans. She wanted to sing about love and breakup, and the hardships faced by those in her Capitol View neighborhood.

"Hmm." Rupert appeared taken aback.

Blaine felt a twinge as he watched the light go out of Naiya's eyes. "I'm sure Naiya isn't planning to go on a diatribe on wax, right?"

She shook her head. "No, it was nothing like that."

Blaine let his eyes dart from Rupert to Naiya. *I hope she knows I'll fight for her to be able to say what she wants to say.* He hadn't fought for Eden back then, and regret had been his constant companion. Fate had seen fit to give him a second chance, perhaps one he didn't even deserve, by sending Naiya his way. *I won't make the same mistake again.*

"Believe me, I understand. We all have things dear to our hearts." Rupert leaned over his desk. "But in this business, it's best not to burn bridges before we've started the journey."

Naiya's voice was quiet. "I understand."

"I'm sure we'll come to a compromise, Rupert. Naiya and I will work with a songwriter to bring out the nuance of her message without getting too controversial."

As Naiya and Rupert walked toward the door, Blaine stood.

Rupert held up his hand. "Hang tight. Marvin wants to speak with you. You can meet Naiya and me in the lobby afterward."

"Sure thing." He watched the two of them disappear into the marbled corridor, wondering what Marvin wanted to talk to him about. As label liaison, Marvin Samuels stayed in frequent contact with him, and Blaine assumed it was that way for all the smaller labels under Hamilton House's umbrella.

Thinking back on his promise to Rupert to get the right songwriter for Naiya's album, he realized he'd not been completely honest. He'd said he had several songwriters in mind, but in reality, there was only one name rolling around in his mind.

Eden Voss.

She'd been dominating his thoughts, and not just because of his fascination with her. Eden was as brilliant a songwriter as Naiya was a vocalist, having written a few charting R & B and hip-hop songs. He'd followed her career closely, because he and Eden had a history—although not one he was entirely proud of.

Years ago, Eden and the members of her girl group had been on the brink of stardom, and he'd been guiding their career. He'd genuinely liked and respected all three young women, though what he'd had with Eden had been different. Special. Their creative synergy had been nothing short of magic. But their attraction to each other had been even more captivating. His heart had opened to her in a way it hadn't to any other woman, before or since.

I ruined their group. But worse than that, I hurt Eden.

Eden had reminded him of his father, set in his ways, immovable in his opinions of the way things "ought to be." His father's rigidity was the main reason Against the Grain existed. Blaine was the second of Caleb and Addison Woodson's five children, the odd one out. He was the goof-off, the one who could never live up to his father's legend or his elder sister's obedient perfection. So rather than join up with the family business at 404 Sound Recordings, one of Atlanta's oldest and most successful recording studios, he'd struck out on his own to form a small label.

He'd made a selfish choice, driven by his need to be independent of his father. His choice had altered all their futures. Cambria had gone on to solo stardom, but that wasn't the case for Eden or her cousin Ainsley.

Marvin entered, dressed in his usual black slacks and dark blue button-down shirt with the record company logo on the front. "Morning, Blaine. Good to see you again."

"Always a pleasure, Marvin. So, Rupert said you wanted to speak to me." Whatever was up, Blaine wanted to get right to the point so he and Naiya could make their flight back to Atlanta after lunch.

Marvin slipped into the chair next to him. "Right. I wanted to congratulate you. I think Naiya is a great fit for the label."

"I appreciate that." *Okay, so why are we really here?*

"While we're pleased to have Naiya on board, we also have very high expectations for this album. It's been over a year since you've had a top-selling album."

He held back his sigh. The ever-changing nature of the music business forced him to keep up with the tastes of a very fickle audience. Sometimes it felt like trying to take down a buck with foam darts. "We had a lull, but things are coming around again."

"I hope you're right. AMGI is making cutbacks, and the first things to go in times like these are underperforming subsidiaries."

The temperature in the room seemed to climb, and Blaine loosened his tie. "Is that where things stand, Marvin?"

The older man looked solemn. "Unfortunately, yes." He stood, gave Blaine a friendly pat on the back. "I have faith in you. You know what you're doing. But I didn't want you to leave without knowing what's going on."

He released a breath. "Thanks for being candid with me."

Marvin's lips curved beneath his bushy blond mustache. "You can count on me to keep you informed." He glanced at his gold wristwatch, headed for the door. "I've got another meeting. Good seeing you again, Blaine."

"Likewise," he murmured as Marvin exited.

Shit. There goes my plan to slowly work my way back into Eden's good graces. Now it wasn't just Naiya's budding career that was on the line. The very future of Against the Grain, his baby, his livelihood, also hung in the balance. He needed to talk to Eden, and fast.

But after what I did...will she even take my call?

TWO

Friday afternoon, Eden breezed into Blaine's office. She was determined he wouldn't see her sweat, so she kept her outer manner as calm and cool as possible, despite the tangle of emotions raging inside her.

When his receptionist had called her yesterday, she'd been tempted to hang up once she learned the call was on Blaine's behalf. She'd decided against it, however, since the woman had only been doing her job. It didn't surprise her that Blaine hadn't had the guts to call himself. He was the last person she wanted to work with, but she wasn't in a position to be picky about the jobs she took on right now.

She'd just left home, where Cooper lay with a broken leg and lacerations to his torso. Ainsley was taking good care of him, but she still felt terrible about what had happened to him. The storm that passed through earlier in the week had sent a tree crashing through the roof onto the foot of his bed. She was grateful he'd avoided more serious injury. The house hadn't been so lucky. It would take a hell of a lot of money to fix the gaping, tarp-covered breach in her roof.

So here I am, going into a business meeting with the man who broke my heart and ended my singing career. Even Hitchcock couldn't have come up with a twist as epic as this.

The moment she saw Blaine, he commanded her full attention. He stood as she entered the space, adjusting his blazer. She couldn't tell if he was straightening it or taking it off; she felt a little disappointed when she realized it was the former. She would have welcomed a better view of his broad shoulders. The disappointment didn't linger, though; she was too busy letting her hungry eyes devour him like a delicious feast. He'd grown into his handsomeness over the past few years and was even more attractive now. *Wonder if he's grown more selfish, too?*

She was intimately acquainted with the ways of a selfish man…her own father had abandoned her and her mother when she was still very young. The scars of that abandonment still remained, and she tended to mistrust men until they proved themselves.

His edgy sense of style remained, as indicated by his clothes. The metallic silver blazer and crisp white shirt whose top two buttons were left open revealed a thick, beaded silver chain with a lion's head as its centerpiece.

Distressed gray jeans sat low on his waist, displaying the outline of the powerful thighs beneath.

She swallowed. She'd come here with so many things on her mind. Now it was all she could do not to drool.

Damn. Even after what he did to me, I'm still fantasizing about him.

Her gaze swept up again, to his rich brown face and the chin-length black dreadlocks he'd bound in a ponytail at his nape. Above a pair of full lips framed by a neatly trimmed beard, his amber eyes sparkled with the flame of youthful passion.

Forget a snack. This man is a whole meal.

"Eden. It's great to see you." His deep voice seemed to fill the whole room.

"Same here." She knew she should move, but her feet were rooted to the spot. She closed her eyes for a moment, willed herself to take a step. *Get it together, girl. Get it together!*

"Come in, sit down." He gestured, welcoming her into his domain.

His invitation seemed to relieve her immobility. She crossed the room and took her seat in the chair positioned near his desk, trying to shift her gaze. She refused to get caught staring at him. Lucky for her, his walls held plenty of interesting portraits, plaques and other things she could look at other than his face. *He's really updated the decor in here.*

Despite all the room's new trappings, Blaine remained the true showpiece.

Retaking his seat in the big leather chair, he said, "I really appreciate you taking my call—"

She interjected. "You mean, your receptionist's call." If he thought she was going to let that slide, he had another think coming.

He cleared his throat as if he were uncomfortable. "I thought if I called, you'd hang up before I could invite you here."

"I probably would have." She folded her arms over her chest.

A slight frown came over his face, though it didn't detract from his magnetism. "You're not going to make this easy, are you?"

She shrugged. "Why should I?" She cocked her head to the right. "I'm older and wiser now, Blaine. I know exactly what you're capable of, and I'll govern myself accordingly." He had no idea how hard she and Ainsley had to work to hold their little household together. He was born into money and had no clue what it was like to struggle.

He dropped his gaze, shuffling through some papers on his desk. "At any rate, thanks for agreeing to meet with me. I know we didn't part on the best terms the last time we were in this office."

She kept her tone even. "I see you've updated things in here. It looks nice."

"Thank you." He pointed at the window behind him. "Finally got some curtains. You were always on me about it."

She sat back in her chair, resting her purse in her lap as she glanced at the gray-and-white-striped curtains. "It's definitely an improvement."

He watched her for a few silent moments. She met his

eyes, camouflaging her true emotions so he wouldn't see how out of sorts he made her feel. He dragged the contact on just long enough to make her squirm inwardly before he spoke again. "Before we get into the details, I feel like I should start with an apology."

She shook her head. "That's not necessary."

"Just let me explain—"

"I don't want to talk about that." She wasn't going to do this with him today. His betrayal still stung, despite the passage of time, and being in his presence again made her feel as if her fragile heart could shatter again at any moment. But there was no way she would ever reveal that to him. "We're not going to talk about the past, Blaine."

One of his thick brows lifted. "Eden, what happened with you and Ainsley back then…"

She held up her hand to stop him, not wanting to hear whatever weak excuses might come next. "It's ancient history. I'd really prefer to just iron out the details of the job at hand, if you don't mind."

"Okay…if that's what you really want." He reclined in the chair, rubbing his large hands together as he asked, "Have you ever heard of Naiya B.?"

She squinted, turning the name over in her mind. "The name sounds familiar, but I can't place it."

"She's an internet celebrity."

Recognition sparked in her brain, and she snapped her fingers. "I think Ainsley showed me a video of her singing 'Greatest Love of All.'"

He nodded. "That video had over eight hundred thousand views in a week. Anyway, I've recently signed

Naiya to Against the Grain, and we're looking for a songwriter to work with her on her first album."

She tilted her head, frowned. Usually an album was a team effort, involving many writers, along with a bevy of producers, musicians and more. "A songwriter? Why not several?"

"Naiya's voice and her brand demand something truly cohesive. We think we can best accomplish that by having a single songwriter work on the entire album—though we may vary the production team a bit here and there."

"And you think I'm the person for the job."

"Absolutely," he replied. "Naiya has a very clear vision of the sound she wants to achieve, a vision I share. And I can think of no one better to help us bring that sound to life than you."

Eden couldn't deny how his words flattered her. She drew a deep breath and instantly regretted it. His woodsy cologne flooded her senses. The scent, familiar and scintillating, made her think of things she shouldn't be thinking of in a serious business meeting. Like what it would be like to be in his arms, to have that scent clinging to her clothes…her bedsheets…

She exhaled, hoping to quell the effects of the fragrance, and the wearer. "May I ask why you feel that way?" *If he's being honest, he'll have no trouble backing up what he says.* His fineness, delicious scent and sweet words awakened her inside, but that didn't mean she trusted him.

He chuckled. "Fair enough. I've been following your

career over these last several years, since we parted ways."

"Oh, have you?"

"Yes. And that's how I know you've written three top-100 songs on the R & B and hip-hop Hot 100 charts, just in the last four years. You've worked with both music legends and young artists. And you can record demos in full voice, which saves me the trouble of getting a studio singer to do them." He pressed his broad shoulders back, holding her gaze. "You're the total package, Eden. Everything we need to generate brilliant lyrics for Naiya lies within you."

Her mouth fell open, and she snapped it shut. "Wow. You've really been keeping tabs on me, huh?"

"In a sense." He gave her a long, speaking look.

She averted her gaze, not wanting to delve into what his eyes were saying that his mouth wasn't. "I have to be honest with you, Blaine. When I walked out of this office all those years ago, I had no intention of ever working with you again."

His jaw hardened. "Eden, I'm sure you understand my decision was a business one. It wasn't personal."

A bitter laugh echoed inside her mind. *That's precisely the problem with you, Blaine Woodson.* She waved her hand dismissively. "It's water under the bridge. Despite what I intended back then; I have good reason to take this job. That's why I took your call."

"I see. Care to elaborate?"

She shook her head. "I see no reason to go into that. After all, this is a simple business transaction." That's what her head said. Other parts of her said something altogether different, but she ignored those parts—for now. "As far as I'm concerned, a professional arrangement is all we can ever hope to have."

Watching Eden from across his desk, Blaine wondered what was going through her head. He knew damn well what was going through his: wonderment.

How did she get even more beautiful?

Seven years ago, she'd been a young woman in her early twenties, with an easygoing manner and grandiose dreams of music stardom. She had to be about thirty now, and she seemed to possess poise and maturity that amplified her natural outer beauty. She was of average height, though her strappy heels made her a couple of inches taller. As she sat across from him in the curve-hugging red dress, with her luscious lips painted to match, her femininity captivated him. She'd worn her dark, auburn-streaked hair loose, falling in large ringlets around her heart-shaped brown face. With those glittering cocoa eyes locked on him, he found it difficult to focus on business.

"Blaine, did you hear what I said?"

He reached back, wrapping his hand around the base of his bound locs for a moment while he gathered his wits. "Forgive me, I'm about a quart low on caffeine. What did you say?"

She narrowed her eyes. "I said, as far as I'm concerned, a business arrangement is all we can have."

"Ouch." He heard her loud and clear that time, and her words stung. He wasn't sure why; this meeting was supposed to be about business. Yet there was no denying how she moved him. He felt his brow crease. What had possessed her to say that to him? Was she talking about the past? Or was she picking up on how he felt right now? Blaine had always known her to be perceptive. "Where did that come from?"

"I just want to make sure that we're clear, right from the start. Mixing business with pleasure never works out the way it should. I'm not sure if you remember how it went down the last time, so we're just not going to do it."

He tried not to linger on the regret her words dredged up. "Of course, I remember." How could he forget the way she'd affected him; the way goose bumps had risen on his skin when he heard her sing? The way his blood had raced when she kissed him?

She pursed her lips, as if unconvinced. "Then you should be willing to keep things professional between us."

"I respect your stance, Eden."

"Good." She released her grip on her handbag, setting it on the desk before flexing her fingers. "Because if you want to work with me, those are my terms."

He knew she was still displeased with his decision to dump the group and elevate Cambria to the ranks of solo star. *If only there was some way I could make her see, make her understand that I did what I had to do.* He cleared his throat. "Eden, I'm just going to say it. I really need you."

Her eyes widened, her ruby lips forming an O shape.

He continued his declaration before she could read too deeply into his meaning. "This album, and its success, are of particular importance. You are the key to that success. Make no mistake, everything that happens between us will be on your terms."

She huffed out a breath, crossing one long leg over the other. "Really? And why should I believe that? You've blindsided me once before." Her shoulders were tense, her chin lifted in defiance.

"I've never denied that."

"I have to be careful about the projects I take on, Blaine," she told him. "My creativity suffers if I'm not."

"I hear you. And I understand why you might be hesitant to work with me. But there's a lot riding on this album, and I can't afford to act in a way that would jeopardize it." He didn't elaborate on the reasoning behind that; there was no reason she needed to know his company could end up being dropped from Hamilton House.

She shook her head, pressing her lips into a rueful half smile. "There was a lot at stake for me back then, too. But I'll take your word for it."

He sighed. She had good reason for mistrusting him, and they both knew it. His hand had been forced, and he'd tried to explain as much to Eden and Ainsley on that fateful day. But emotions had been too high, and both women had left his office visibly upset.

"I assume you've drawn up a contract?"

He opened his desk drawer and took out the document, sliding it across the desk to her. "Let me know if you need an explanation of anything."

He watched as she perused the document. Moments later, a shocked look passed over her face, but it was gone as quickly as it had appeared.

Silence fell between them while she finished reading

the contract, and he used the time to respond to a few messages on his smartphone. When she looked up, he slid a gold-plated pen toward her.

Shaking her head, she said, "I'll need some time to consider the offer."

His brows hitched. "How much time?"

"Give me a week. I'll definitely make a decision by then." She used her fingertips to roll the pen back toward him.

He reached for the pen before she moved her hand, and their fingers brushed momentarily.

A buzz, like the kick of a finely aged whiskey, fired through his blood. Her skin was as smooth and soft as satin. Even the brief connection was enough to remind him of those long-ago nights they'd spent together in the studio. He hadn't forgotten what they'd shared, and despite her cool manner, he could tell she hadn't forgotten, either.

She drew her hand away, tucking it into her lap and looking away from him.

She felt it, too.

He returned the pen to his drawer. "If you decide to sign the contract, we'll be able to give you a check for half the fee."

She nodded, dropping her shoulders, her rigid posture relaxing. When she spoke again, her tone had softened, lacking the earlier edginess. "Sounds good. If I take the job, when do we get started?"

It pleased him that she seemed more at ease. "I'd like to have you meet with Naiya and me next Monday, if possible. Would that work?"

"That would be fine. What's the time and place?"

"Here, in the conference room, about ten."

She stood. "Is there anything else?"

There's plenty. But now wasn't the time. She'd placed a wall between them for her own protection, and despite his fierce attraction to her, he'd always respect her boundaries. "No, that's all. Thank you again for coming, and for considering the offer."

"Just don't make me regret it, Blaine." She gave him a soft smile, turned and walked out of his office, leaving her parting words hanging in the air like a fog.

Three

Saturday morning, Eden sat beside Ainsley in the waiting room of the children's specialty clinic. On the opposite side of Ainsley, Cooper dozed, his head resting on his mother's shoulder.

"He's been in and out of sleep since we left the house," Eden noted, gesturing to her slumbering little nephew. Normally Cooper was a ball of unfettered energy, so seeing him napping in public like a worn-out toddler was a bit jarring for her.

Ainsley nodded. "It's the pain meds they gave him. The ER doc said they'd make him drowsy, remember?" She didn't remember, actually, but didn't see the need to say that aloud. Between the tree falling on the roof, spending the better part of Saturday at the emergency room with Cooper and then meeting up with Blaine on Friday, the last several days had been a blur of unpleasant surprises.

"You never really told me about your meeting with—" Ainsley fluttered her lashes dramatically "—Blaine yesterday."

She rolled her eyes. "Why are you saying his name like that?"

"I'm just teasing you, girl." She giggled. "I know you hate his guts."

"Don't you?" She gave her cousin a penetrating stare. "I'm sure you remember him holding your child against you."

Ainsley shrugged. "He's not my favorite person in the world, but I don't hate him, either. And if I had to do it all again, I'd still choose my son over a music career, so…"

Eden shook her head. "You've got Aunt Mimi's forgiving spirit."

"And you've got your mama's sass." Ainsley winked. "But seriously, how did the meeting go?"

"I don't really want to talk about it." She had no interest in telling her cousin that she'd spent the better part of their meeting willing herself not to drool over Blaine's dreadlocked handsomeness. Or that he'd smelled like freshly minted cash and great sex. Nope, she'd keep that to herself. At least for now.

"Oh, come on." Ainsley nudged her with an elbow. "At least tell me if you took the gig."

She sighed. "I asked him to give me until next Monday to make my decision. But—"

A loud voice called out Cooper's name, effectively

ending the conversation. Ainsley raised her hand, waving the scrub-clad nurse over. Silently blessing the timing, Eden helped rouse Cooper and hoist him to a standing position. Between their supportive arms, the nurse holding doors and his crutches, they finally got him back to the examination room.

Eden settled into a chair across from Ainsley after they'd helped Cooper onto the bed. Immediately taking out her phone, she gave rapt attention to her social media feed, as a sign to her cousin that she didn't want to talk.

Soon, Dr. Celia Fordham entered the room. Petite and slender, she wore her dark hair in a bun low on her nape. Adjusting the oval frames of her glasses, she asked, "How are you feeling today, Cooper?"

"My leg itches," he groused. "I can't scratch it 'cause of the cast."

Dr. Fordham smiled. "Don't worry, that's pretty typical." Giving him a pat on the shoulder, she asked, "Any pain?"

Cooper nodded his head. "How long will I have to wear this thing, Doc?"

"I'm afraid it could take about six weeks for your leg to fully heal."

Cooper's eyes grew round. "Six weeks? But baseball tryouts will be over by then!"

Dr. Fordham turned to Ainsley. "Tryouts?"

"He's going to middle school this year, and he wants to try to make the team. It's all he's talked about for the last two years."

Cooper nodded. "Yeah. That's why I gotta get out of this cast."

Eden sighed. The timing of this little disaster couldn't have been worse. Money was lean around the household, and now Cooper was faced with missing out on something he desperately wanted.

"I'm sorry, Cooper. But with this cast on, you won't be able to…"

Tears gathered in his eyes. "But I have to! I've been waiting forever to play on the baseball team."

Ainsley, visibly emotional, went to her son's side. Draping her arm around his shoulders, she asked, "Isn't there something else we can do for him, Dr. Fordham?"

"Yes, actually, there is another option. For the type of fracture Cooper has, surgery is a possibility. With him being as young and healthy as he is, I don't see why he couldn't get back on his feet in time for his tryouts." Dr. Fordham took the clipboard from beneath her arm, flipping through the pages. "If you like, I could put in a recommendation for the procedure."

"What would it entail, exactly?" Eden asked.

Dr. Fordham gave a brief rundown of what the surgery would involve.

Ever practical, Ainsley queried, "Will insurance cover this?"

Dr. Fordham appeared thoughtful. "It should cover at least a portion, but you'll have to check with the insurance clerk at checkout to be certain."

Ainsley looked thoughtful for a moment, but by the time they left the clinic, Dr. Fordham had put in an order for the procedure.

Eden drove her cousin and nephew home. The silence that had stretched on for the ten minutes since they'd left the hospital was starting to get to her. Her mind kept drifting to Blaine, and he was a distraction she just didn't need right now. So, she asked, "When are we going to talk about this surgery, Ainsley?"

"What about it?"

She scoffed. "Come on, Ainsley. You heard the clerk. We have to meet a two-thousand-dollar deductible in order for insurance to pay for the surgery. How are we gonna afford that?"

"I'll figure it out. Besides, I've already paid five hundred."

"No, *we* will figure it out, stubborn. That's still fifteen hundred dollars, and I'm not going to let you try to come up with all that cash on your own. We're family, and I'm here for you."

Ainsley blew out a breath. "I couldn't say no to him, Eden. Not with him giving me those big sad puppy eyes."

She nodded. "I know. As I said, we'll figure it out together."

Decision made, silence fell between them. Her eyes on the road, Eden thought back to her meeting with Blaine. She had not given him a definite response, but there was no turning down the gig now, no matter how much she disliked being in Blaine's company. The fee she'd make would cover Cooper's medical bills, and hopefully, the roof repair.

"So, is this a better time to ask what happened with Blaine?"

She sighed. "No. But I don't think there ever will be."

Ainsley chuckled. "Just spill it already."

Reluctantly, she recounted the details of their meeting. "Anyway, I'm looking forward to working with Naiya. She's very talented."

"Mmm-hmm."

She eyed her cousin. "What, Ainsley?"

"Well, you left out the most important part." Her cousin scratched her chin. "Is he still as fine as he used to be?"

"Honestly? He's finer." She turned the wheel to the left, navigating into their driveway. "Not that it matters. All interactions between Blaine and me will be strictly business. We've already discussed it."

But even as she said the words, deep down she knew that arrangement might be hard to keep.

Holding his briefcase over his head to shield himself from the pounding rain, Blaine dashed into the Bodacious Bean Thursday morning. Once inside, he scanned the interior while walking toward the counter. His younger brother Gage was due to meet him there for a quick chat, and he didn't want to spend too long lingering in the coffee shop. Despite the colorful HBCU-themed decor, friendly staff and inviting atmosphere, Blaine had far too much work to do in preparing for Naiya B.'s album to be hanging out here all day. Grabbing a few napkins to wipe the droplets clinging to his face and his briefcase, he stepped up to place his order.

By the time the barista set to work on his large French vanilla latte, the bell rang over the door, indicating the entry of another patron. Blaine turned toward the sound and smiled when he saw Gage shut his umbrella and shake it before ducking inside.

"How you doing, bro?" Blaine asked.

Shaking his head, Gage wiped a hand over his damp forehead. Dressed in a charcoal-gray suit, crisp white shirt and purple tie, he didn't look too pleased about the numerous wet spots covering his clothing. "Pretty good, considering this torrential downpour." He gestured to the window, where rain continued to pelt the glass.

"Gotta love that ATL weather. One day chicken, next day feathers." Blaine chuckled as he took his drink from the barista. "I'll grab us a table in the back." He walked away, leaving his soggy brother at the counter.

The place was pretty empty for a weekday morning. *Guess the rain kept them away.* Blaine usually got his coffee to go, because open tables were scarce most workdays. Finding a suitable two-top table near the establishment's rear window, he sat down, easing the briefcase beneath the table. Watching the falling rain, he sipped from his sleeve-wrapped paper cup, enjoying the feel of the warm, slightly sweet beverage as it washed over his tongue.

Gage set his cup down. "So, what's going on? I figured you needed something when you asked me to meet in the middle of the workweek."

"I do need a favor, but we'll get to that." He rested his hands on the table, lacing his fingers together. Despite the tense relationship he had with his family, he still cared about them. "How's the fam?"

Gage rolled his eyes. "Our siblings are fine. It's

pretty much business as usual with them. Dad's been complaining about his tennis elbow acting up for almost two weeks but refuses to go to the doctor. That leaves the rest of us stuck listening to his gripes."

He wasn't surprised by his brother's observation. Their father wasn't one to admit defeat, and he'd likely go on bearing the pain until it became so bad he was forced to seek medical attention. "Dad's always been like that. What about Mom?"

"She's great. Still all about fitness. She's vegan now, did you know that?"

He shook his head. "How long has that been a thing?"

"A month or so. And she's moved on from step aerobics to kickboxing." Gage snorted a laugh, took another sip of his coffee. "We all try to stay on her good side because it's pretty obvious she can kick all of our asses."

Blaine couldn't help smiling at his brother's words. *Mom's always been a pistol.* "She may just outlive us all." He finished up his drink, setting the empty cup aside. "So, what's up at 404? Everything good business-wise?"

"Yeah. We're still solidly in the black. We're looking to update some things, though. First is that equipment in Studio A. I think Dad kept it so long because it was his first soundboard—you know, sentimental attachment or something. But that thing's long overdue for an upgrade."

"And as head of operations, that falls under your jurisdiction." He watched his brother intently. "What are you going to do with the old equipment?" He was somewhat surprised his father had agreed to part with it, though he assumed their brother Miles, who served as finance officer, had explained how new equipment would bring higher profits into the studio.

Gage tilted his head to one side. "For right now, it's going into storage. After that, who knows? We may donate it to a museum, though Mom's been talking about setting up a display in the building to commemorate the thirtieth anniversary. So, we'll see."

He nodded but remained silent.

"You know, you could always come by the offices and *see* your family, instead of always asking me how everyone is." Gage gave him a pointed look.

"And you know why I can't do that." He was in no mood to talk about the rift between him and his family. He was the black sheep, the wayward son who'd gone off on his own instead of joining the family business. He missed his mother, and would occasionally text her, as well as his baby sister, Teagan. But everyone else sided with his father, so what was there for them to discuss? "I'm not into drama, Gage. So, I avoid it whenever possible."

"Hmph." A slight frown tilted his baby bro's lips, but it disappeared as quickly as it had shown itself. "Anyway, let's get to the matter at hand. What's going on with you? Because I hear you're doing big things."

His brow furrowed as he asked, "What have you heard?"

"I heard you nabbed that hot viral video singer for your label."

Blaine smiled. "Oh, so you heard about Naiya B.? I'm glad she's a hot topic around town."

"I've heard her sing, and I must say, she's quite a score. Congrats, bro."

"Thanks. She's got an amazing voice. Songwriting isn't her strength, but I've come up with a brilliant solution to that problem."

Gage's expression morphed from curiosity into a knowing grin. "I heard about that, too. When were you going to tell me you had a meeting with Eden Voss?"

Blaine let his head drop back. "Damn, bro. You're really all up in my business like that?"

He shrugged. "Come on, B. You know how word gets around in southwest Atlanta. I'm just mad I had to hear it in these SWATS streets instead of from you."

Blaine groaned.

Gage leaned in, his tone low and conspiratorial. "So, y'all just working together? Or are y'all…*working together*?" He waggled his brows to accentuate the last two words.

Blaine resisted the urge to pop his brother upside the head. "Ugh, Gage. You're so freaking annoying. It's a business arrangement, bruh. I offered Eden a contract to write some songs for Naiya. Hopefully she'll sign, and we'll all get paid. That's it."

Gage gave him that familiar head tilt/side-eye combo, the one that meant he didn't believe what he'd heard. "Oh, really?"

"Yes, really. It's. Strictly. Business. Case closed."

"You're awfully touchy about it for that to be true… but I'll take your word for it." They chatted for a few moments about Blaine's possible use of 404's live band recording studio, and how Blaine could do his usual "wear a hoodie and use the rear entrance" routine to keep his father from being aware of his presence.

"Yeah, yeah." Gage crushed his empty paper cup, tossing it into the nearby trash can. "You know, you and Dad are going to have to iron things out eventually."

"I know, I know." *But not yet.*

Four

Eden entered the modest one-story building that housed Against the Grain Records on Monday morning, carrying her leather-bound notebook and purse. Inside, she took a few steps toward the waiting area, consisting of chairs and a low black enamel coffee table. Resting her palm on the cool steel frame, she took a seat in one of the sleek black leather chairs, intent on mentally preparing herself for the day ahead.

She crossed one leg over the other, taking a good look around. She'd been anxious the first time she met Blaine here, so she relished the opportunity to evaluate his domain. The roomy space, with its stained concrete floors, soft gray walls and black lacquer furniture, was an obvious reflection of his tastes. Framed black-and-white prints of musicians playing instruments adorned the walls, and the reception desk was flanked by two polished pewter sculptures: one of a bass clef, the other, a treble clef.

She liked the decor; it was simple, well-coordinated and reflective of the type of business conducted there. Back in the day, Blaine's studio had been little more than a desk and chair surrounded by blank walls. Now he had made the space his own. He'd obviously experienced some degree of success during their time apart.

If only he'd afforded Ainsley and I that same chance at success. After all that had transpired between them, she never would have expected to find herself working with him at this point in her life. But fate obviously had other plans.

Back then, she'd been so enamored with him that she could never have anticipated his betrayal. He'd seemed so perfect, so loving and so into her. He'd taken her hand and touched her soul.

She sighed as the image of his drop-dead-gorgeous face floated through her mind. As enticing as he was, however, she knew she had to get her mind right for the task ahead. Daydreaming about Blaine simply wouldn't do.

I've got to get focused. There's so much at stake.

Her professional reputation aside, she had about as much motivation to succeed at this job as a person could have. She'd agreed to split the fees for Cooper's surgery with Ainsley, and she knew she'd need to replace the $1,250 she took from her savings. Beyond that, the damage to their roof was so extensive, she'd need an entirely new one, to the tune of $6,500 above what her homeowner's policy covered.

She massaged her temple, blowing out a breath. *It's not just about Naiya's album anymore. I need to do well with this project because if I do, it will open up the door to so many more opportunities.*

The door swung open then, and she turned her head. As the blast of humid August air ruffled her bangs, Blaine strode in.

Her breath caught in her throat at the sight of him. He wore a loose-fitting pair of blue jeans, a black Goodie Mob tee, and black-and-white leather sneakers. A denim jacket was draped over his broad shoulders, Georgia heat be damned. His dreads were in a bun atop his head, and dark sunglasses obscured his eyes.

No one had a right to be so freaking handsome. And yet there he stood, looking like temptation personified. Liquid desire pooled low in her belly, the warmth spreading through her body. She took a deep breath. *Gather yourself, girl. He's just a man.*

She stood, brushing remnants of this morning's biscuit from the front of her dark skirt. "Good morning, Blaine."

He smiled, teeth glistening. "Good morning, Eden." He leaned down, and before she could react, pecked her on the cheek. "So, I'm assuming you decided to sign the contract?"

Heat bloomed beneath her skin. Doing her best to shake off the effects of his disarming smile and his surprise kiss, she handed him the document. "Yes. I'll do my best to live up to your expectations."

"I have no doubt that you will." A sparkle lit his dark eyes.

Naiya entered the room then, a bright smile on her face. "Morning, folks."

Gathering her wits, Eden moved past Blaine to greet the vocalist. Sticking out her hand, she said, "Naiya, I'm Eden Voss. It's nice to finally meet you in person."

Naiya offered a small smile and handshake. "Thanks. Nice to meet you, too."

Dressed in a simple green sundress and a pair of tan sandals, with her flowing, blond-streaked brown waves of hair hanging loose around her shoulders, the petite young woman appeared somewhat nervous. Eden noticed the way her eyes darted around the space, never settling in any one place for long.

Blaine removed his shades, his dark eyes shimmering with a mixture of confidence and mischief. "Now that you two ladies have met, let's get to work on this album, shall we?" He winked, then began walking past the reception desk and down the hall.

Eden swallowed. Those piercing eyes…deep brown, flecked with gold. They'd been her downfall once before, and she couldn't afford another fall. Not now. She dragged her gaze away from him, focusing on Naiya. Looping her arm through the younger woman's, she asked, "Tell me about your vision for this album."

A few minutes later, they were settled into the recording studio. Blaine sat at the control board, while Naiya and Eden sat facing each other inside the booth. As Naiya relayed some of the topics she wanted to explore on her album, Eden took notes. Listening to Naiya,

Eden found herself increasingly intrigued by the young singer's words. Not only was she a talented vocalist, but she possessed great intellect, as well as a surprising level of awareness of the world around her.

"I have to tell you, Naiya. I was impressed with your singing, but now that I've heard your thoughts, I'm even more impressed with you." Eden closed her notebook, resting it on her lap. "You're so tuned in to everything."

Naiya tilted her head to one side, releasing a brief giggle. "I know people like to think that the younger generation is too self-absorbed to notice such things. But not all of us are that way."

Eden winced, noticing the way Naiya had subtly quashed her preconceived notions. "I can see that. And I'm honored to help you realize your vision with this album."

Naiya snapped her fingers as if remembering something. "I almost forgot. I brought my journal." She reached into her purse, taking out a small spiral-bound book and passing it to her. "I don't know what your process is like, but I thought it might help with the lyrics."

Accepting the journal, Eden smiled. "It absolutely will help. Thank you for trusting me with it."

Blaine's voice filled the booth as he spoke into the mic. "Okay, ladies. Have you had enough time to chat?"

They both nodded.

"Good," he continued. "The bigwigs at the label want us to turn around a first single pretty quickly, so we need to get cracking on that. After that's done, we'll tackle the rest of the album."

Naiya's grin revealed her excitement. Standing, she

slipped on a headset and spoke into the mic. "Do we have a beat yet?"

"Yep. Just got one in from Jazzy." Blaine flipped a few switches on the soundboard, and the sounds of the track filled the space.

Eden was bobbing her head and tapping her foot almost immediately, and she felt the smile sweeping over her face. The track sounded unique and fresh, yet reminiscent of nineties hip-hop. "This is fantastic."

Naiya, snapping along with the beat, said, "You can't go wrong with an 808. I love this! It's retro but it's current at the same time."

Eden had to agree. The Roland TR-808 drum machine had played a seminal role in hip hop and R & B music, starting with its release in 1980. While it was only in production for three years, the 808 had been used for countless hit songs, and even today's music software often emulated the patterns the legendary drum machine had created. The track the producer had created for Naiya had just enough instrumentality to give it a classic sound and used the 808 to lay down a trap drum line popularized by some of the hottest recent rap acts.

Blaine's million-dollar smile beamed through the glass partition. "Great. Then it'll give y'all the perfect jumping-off point. I'll just let it loop." He slid back from the board and stood.

Eden turned his way, and their eyes connected.

He offered her a smile tinged with wickedness.

Her breath caught in her throat. She could remember him smiling at her, just that way, one night when they'd been working together. She swallowed, recalling how that smile had set off a chain of events that had ended with them making love. Her tongue darted over her lower lips as she recalled the way he'd bent her over the conference room table and lifted her skirt...

His voice cut into her memories. "I'll be in my office. I've got a call to make." Taking off his headset, he exited the studio with a wave.

Eden watched him go, feeling a mixture of relief and disappointment as his overpowering male energy left the space. She knew she needed him gone so she could concentrate, yet less logical parts of her wanted him nearby.

In the quiet of his office, Blaine sat down at his desk and sighed. He hated to leave the studio, because he loved watching the creative process in real time. It was like being present for a birth, metaphorically speaking. There was nothing else quite like watching a musician bring forth a new song. The music became a living thing with a bass line for a pulse, a lyrical heart and a body made of sound. Out in the world, that music could change someone's mood, their day or even the trajectory of their life.

He believed in the transformative power of music. To him, it was just as tangible and present as the air he breathed or the water he drank. That was why he'd entered the music business. It wasn't about the storied Woodson family and their history. It was about him, pursuing his true calling, on his own terms.

And now, to be working with Eden again felt amazing. She'd been his muse in the past, and he knew she'd be able to create something truly special with Naiya. A tiny part of him still held out hope that she'd create something special with him, too, something as beautiful and as timeless as a classic love song. He knew it would take work to get back into her heart, but he was willing to do whatever it took.

Marvin's cryptic warning from their meeting in New York had been echoing in his head. In order for him to move forward with Naiya's debut, he needed to know the whole story. Parts of him were ill at ease, and he hesitated over the keypad of his phone.

But he pushed past his apprehension and dialed his boss's direct number.

A few moments later, he ended the call. Leaning back in his chair, he released the groan he'd been holding back for most of the call. In a way, he'd expected bad news. But he'd never thought it would be this serious. The sweeping changes being made by AMGI made him nervous. And even if Against the Grain survived this round of cuts, what guarantee did he have that he wouldn't be facing the same situation again at some point in the future?

The other blow from the call was Marvin's admission that label management wasn't fully on board with his decision to have Eden do all the songwriting. According to the suits, Eden didn't have a consistent enough track record for writing chart toppers.

He sighed. *What I really need is a massively successful album. With that kind of money, I could cut ties with*

the corporate world of music, and Against the Grain
would become a truly independent label.

Maybe Naiya's album would be just what Against
the Grain needed.

He thought of the other three artists he was currently
working with, but none of them seemed more likely than
Naiya to deliver the powerhouse content he needed.

You could just ask your father for help, a voice in the
recesses of his mind chided.

He frowned, rejecting that voice. He'd made it this
far without his father's money, and there was no way
he'd ask for it now.

Pushing his chair back from the desk, he stood and
stretched. Eden and Naiya were probably well into their
process by now, and even though he wasn't in the best
mood, he wanted to observe as much of it as he could.
Pocketing his phone, he left his office.

Instead of returning to the studio, he exited the building via the rear door and headed for the small courtyard.
After the conversation he'd just had, he needed some
fresh air and some time to clear his head before he went
back to working the controls. As he moved toward the
wrought iron bench beneath the old poplar tree, he noticed someone sitting there.

Eden. The sight of her made his pulse race.

A smile turned up the corners of his mouth as he
approached her. "What brings you out here, Eden?"

She looked up from her phone, a soft smile on her
face. "I...couldn't focus. So, I decided to come outside
and get a little fresh air."

He chuckled. "What a coincidence. I'm in need of a little decompression myself."

"The music biz." She shook her head, her gaze directed upward, as if she were studying the canopy of leaves above her head. "It's not for the faint of heart."

"That's for sure." He moved closer, gesturing to the empty spot next to her. "Mind if I join you?"

She was quiet for a moment. Just before the silence became uncomfortably long, she said, "Go ahead."

He sat next to her, leaving only a sliver of space between them. Draping his arm over the back of the bench, he asked, "How far have you two gotten on the single?"

"Not very. I know the direction for the song, but I was feeling a bit stuck." She ran a hand over her loose curls. "I thought it would be better to just take some time and get myself together, rather than try to force the process, ya know?"

He nodded. "I get it." He scratched his chin with his free hand. "Do you remember that time back in the day when you had writer's block? We were working on that song 'Love by Night.'"

She tilted her head, looked thoughtful. A moment later, she snapped her fingers. "Yeah, I remember. That's the time we went for that run around Piedmont Park, right?"

"Right."

She let her head fall back against his arm as she laughed. "Oh, man. I had forgotten about that."

"You wanna go for a run now?" He gave her a teasing look.

She rolled her eyes. "You know the answer to that." Gesturing to her body, she said, "I don't run, and it's probably obvious."

"I can tell you still work out, though." He winked. "I know it takes effort to maintain a shape like that."

Her cheeks reddened as she changed the subject. "How long is that trail loop? Three miles?"

"Closer to four. It was a hell of a workout."

She laughed. "You're telling me. I remember going back to the studio sore and sweaty."

He leaned in, unable to resist. "Do you think that was because of the actual run? Or what we did on the trail?"

She dropped her gaze to her lap.

"Remember? We found that little wooded nook just off the path…" He traced his fingertip in a circle over her thigh.

Her hand went to her chest, and she swallowed hard. "I remember, Blaine."

"Standing in that position for so long might have made you sore," he announced. "But I never heard any complaints."

"I didn't have any," she admitted softly. "It was amazing…you were amazing."

Their gazes met, and the heat of the memories they'd made in that little corner of the park passed between them. He could still hear her soft moans, feel her hands grasping his shoulders for purchase as he tasted the sweetness flowing between her thighs.

He picked up her hand, raising it to his lips. Placing a soft kiss against her palm, he released her. "We'd better go back inside." It was true…he knew that if they remained out here much longer, he wouldn't be able to resist dragging her soft, curvy body into his lap.

She stood, appearing a little shaky on her feet, but only for a moment. "Agreed." After a moment's hesitation, she added, "Blaine, we really shouldn't dwell on the past now. Let's just keep things professional, okay?"

He offered a quick nod in response.

Seconds later she walked past him. Enjoying the view of her backside, he followed her back into the building.

Five

The next day, Eden was back in her seat on the stool inside the recording studio at Against the Grain. Her leather notebook on her lap, she absently flipped through the pages. Naiya's journal had proven to be a valuable resource for Eden when it came to writing lyrics for her debut single.

I just hope I'm going in the right direction for Naiya. She certainly has a lot to say.

With the wealth of information she'd gleaned about the singer's inner life, she felt confident that she'd written a solid draft for the single. Now it was simply a matter of whether Naiya and Blaine agreed.

Thinking of Blaine brought a slight smile to her lips, despite her better judgment. She still remembered the day they'd met on the campus of Atlanta Tech. He'd been charming, funny and easygoing, and at the time, she'd thought him the perfect counter to her studious, hardworking, straitlaced self. Blaine Woodson wasn't like any other man she'd ever met, and he'd fascinated her from the very start. What followed could only be described as a passionate affair. While they worked on music in the studio, their hearts entwined like the treble and bass lines of a song. Their song was beautiful, yet tragically brief.

With time came wisdom, though, and she'd since learned the folly of her ways. What had seemed like an ideal match had only led to heartbreak for her, both romantically and professionally. Shaking her head to cast off those wayward thoughts, she stood. Leaving her notebook on the stool, she left the studio and went across to the ladies' room.

When she returned to the studio and opened the door, she detected a familiar woodsy and decidedly masculine aroma. As she entered the space, a small creaking sound near the board drew her attention. She glanced in the direction of the sound and saw Blaine sitting there, his back to her as he spun the chair slightly from side to side.

She cleared her throat, and as he pivoted to face her, plastered on a congenial smile. "Hi, Blaine. How are you?"

"I'm fine. Much better now that you're here." He grinned. "I'm excited to see what you've come up with, and I'm sure Naiya is, as well."

She answered only with a smile and a nod. She didn't open her mouth, to avoid saying something foolish.

What was it about his presence, the sound of his voice, that made her knees go weak? She looked through the glass partition, and seeing no one in the booth, asked, "Where is Naiya, anyway?"

"Caught in traffic. She texted me to let me know she's on her way."

She chuckled. "Gotta love Atlanta traffic."

"Yeah. Where the rush hour is from midnight to 11:59 p.m." He scoffed. "I've been late to many an appointment trying to navigate through Midtown."

"You've actually got a better shot getting places on time if you walk." As much as she loved the city and her fellow "ATLiens," she didn't think she'd ever get used to the frenetic pace of traffic, especially 85 where it cut through the heart of the city.

He rubbed his hands together. "So, you ready to get this single done?"

"I am, assuming you and Naiya like the lyrics I've come up with."

"Can I take a look?"

She shook her head. "I always let the artist lay eyes on my lyrics first. After Naiya's seen it, then you can take a look."

He looked surprised but seemed to take it in stride. "Okay. Can't blame me for being curious, though. There's a lot riding on this album."

She watched him silently, noting the way his entire demeanor changed when he uttered the last few words. *There's a lot riding on this album.* Was that indicative of the way he felt about every album his label released?

Or was there something more to the story, something she wasn't privy to?

Before she could ask any more questions, a smiling Naiya entered. Her hair was in a ponytail hanging down the back of her pink-and-white maxi dress. "Hey, y'all."

"Hi, Naiya." Eden turned her full attention to the young singer. "I'm really excited for you to see what I've come up with for your first single."

She clapped her hands together. "Me, too. Let's dig in."

The two women entered the booth and took their seats. Eden hazarded a quick glance through the glass partition and saw Blaine leaning his elbows on the soundboard surround. The expression on his face looked as if his mind was elsewhere. Returning her focus to Naiya, Eden handed over her leather notebook. "Here's the song. After reading your journal, I thought your first love might be a good place to start."

Naiya blew out a breath. "So, we're going for drama, eh?"

"Sort of. Anyway, I think the things you wrote about your first love and the subsequent heartbreak were very compelling. Audiences are pretty likely to relate to that, regardless of their age."

"I hope you're right."

Eden watched as Naiya read through the lyrics. "Trust me on this one. Love songs usually take one of two paths. Romantic and sentimental, or bitter breakup. What I've tried to do is create a third path. 'It didn't work out, but I don't hate you, and you gave me some good memories.'"

Naiya nodded. "Nice."

Silence fell between them, and Eden thought about the lyrics she'd written. The story had not only been inspired by the words in Naiya's journal, but by her own experience with Blaine. They'd had a great time way back when, and though she doubted she'd ever fully trust him again, she didn't hate him. On the contrary, she wished him happiness.

I just wonder if he could ever find that happiness with me. Thinking about all she'd shared with him was bittersweet. There were parts of her heart, hidden deep down where no one could see, that still craved his love. But logic and common sense told her to steer clear of him. Working with him, while keeping things strictly professional, proved more challenging than she would have expected.

Naiya looked up from the notebook, her eyes wide.

Eden watched warily, unsure of what her expression meant. "What do you think?"

"Wow." Naiya shook her head from side to side. "This song…is fantastic."

Releasing a pent-up breath, Eden remarked, "Awesome. Your expression had me a little worried there."

"I'm just amazed at how accurately you captured my sentiments about my first love." She held up the notebook. "It's not sappy and fake, nor is it ragey and bitter. It really toes the perfect line."

Placing her hand over her heart, she smiled. "Thank you. It means a lot to me that you like it."

"We're going to work great together." Naiya's gaze dropped to the handwritten lyrics again. "I can tell."

Eden spun halfway around on the stool, intent on knocking on the glass to get Blaine's attention. When she faced the partition, she saw him standing near the studio's open door, talking animatedly to a very familiar-looking man.

Naiya asked, "Who's that Blaine is speaking with?"

Eden shrugged. "One of his brothers, though I'm not sure which one." She watched the exchange, and even though the booth's soundproofing prevented her from hearing their conversation, she could tell by their body language that their discussion was heated.

Blaine threw up his hands and returned to the sound-board. Engaging the mic, he said, "Ladies, I need to go to my office for a bit. I'll be back as soon as I can."

Without waiting for a response, he switched off the mic and strode from the room.

Eden blew out a breath. *What's going on with him?* When they'd been in the studio alone, she'd had his full attention. Now it was obvious something else was at play, and she couldn't help feeling frustrated. "Okay, then. I guess we're working on paper for a bit. Any tweaks you want to make to the lyrics?"

Stalking down the hallway toward his office, Blaine stopped near the benches outside his door. Gage, following close behind him, nearly collided with him.

Fixing his brother with a hard stare, he asked, "Why in the hell would you do this, Gage? Why would you bring Dad here?"

"Because he asked me to." Gage shook his head.

"More like he demanded it. What did you expect me to do?"

"Show some backbone and tell him no," he groused. "We're not kids anymore, Gage. We don't have to do everything he says."

Gage ran a hand over his close-trimmed fade. "Maybe you aren't, bro. But in case you forgot, my office is two doors down from his. The only way I was going to be left alone to get my work done was if I did what he asked."

Blaine sighed. "Thanks a lot, Gage."

"You're welcome. He's in your office, and I'd suggest you don't keep him waiting much longer."

Groaning, Blaine went to his office door. He leaned forward, peering through the small tempered-glass window.

Just as Gage had said, Caleb Woodson sat in the guest chair near Blaine's desk. Blaine could see his father's sour disposition displayed on his bearded face. Caleb wore one of the charcoal Italian-cut suits he favored, and his arms were folded over his chest.

Pausing to take a deep, steadying breath, he turned the knob and pushed it open. "Good morning, Father."

"Hmph. What's so good about it?" Caleb's gruff tone communicated the same level of dissatisfaction as his expression. "Come on in here. I need to talk to you."

Blaine let the door shut behind him, seeing no reason to subject the whole building to their discussion. Walking around the desk, he took a seat and faced his ornery father. "Well, it must be important. I never expected you'd lower yourself to visit me here." He knew his words were harsh, but they were also true. His father had basically disowned him when he'd opened Against the Grain. "You could have called, so you wouldn't have to sully yourself."

"Trust me, son, I don't want to be here any more than you want to see me." Caleb leaned forward, placing his hands atop the desk and lacing his fingers together. "The only reason I came here instead of calling is that I wanted to see your face when I asked you this question. That way I'll know if you're lying to me."

He wanted to roll his eyes but refrained. "Go ahead. Ask away."

"What do you know about Hamilton House putting in a bid to buy out 404 Sound?"

Blaine furrowed his brow. "Dad, what are you talking about?"

Caleb watched him intently, his dark eyes boring into his son's. "You mean you haven't heard anything about your principal backers trying to take over my life's work?"

He sighed. "No, Dad. I don't know anything about it."

"Are you sure? Weren't you in New York at the headquarters not too long ago?"

"Yes, I was in New York recently," Blaine retorted. "But I don't know anything about this whole buyout situation. What you just told me is the first time I've heard it."

Caleb watched him for a few seconds more. Letting his shoulders droop, he took his hands off the desk and sat back in his chair. "I see."

"I'm not sure what kind of relationship you think I have with Hamilton House, but it's not like I'm privy to every decision they make." Blaine rubbed his temples, feeling a headache coming on. "They help fund my business, and in exchange, they get a cut of my profits. That's the entire extent of our relationship."

Caleb rubbed his hands together. "Would you have told me if you knew about it?"

He shrugged. "I don't know. It's not really my place."

His father shook his head, his expression grim. "You're such a disappointment, Blaine. I wanted so much more for you."

There it is. Dad can't talk to me for more than five minutes without taking a shot at me. Shaking his head at the patronizing tone his father had taken, he sighed. "I know, Dad. And I'm sorry I can't be as perfectly organized as Nia, or as obedient as Gage and Miles, or as creative as Teagan. I'm the family screw-up, and if I ever forget that, I'll always have you to remind me, won't I?"

"Not always, kid." His lips twisted into a grimace. "But that's neither here nor there."

"Nice use of guilt there, Dad. You missed your calling as an actor on a daytime soap."

Caleb slammed his fist on the table. "Watch your tone, Blaine. I'm still your father."

He averted his eyes, remaining silent. As strained as their relationship was, he didn't set out to purposely disrespect his father.

"You listen, and you listen good. Addy and I raised all our children with good manners and good sense. You're grown now, and your choices are your own. But don't you sit there acting like you sprouted up from the earth fully formed. Show some damn respect."

"I'm sorry, Dad," he murmured. "It's just that I did all this for myself." He gestured around the office. "I did it on my own, and you never give me credit for it."

"Yes, son, you did do this on your own. Against my advice and without my blessing. And I admit you've done all right for yourself. But had you stayed with 404, stayed with the family, you'd be doing better."

Blaine blew out an aggravated breath. "Okay, Dad. I've answered your question, so can I get back to running my business now?"

Caleb stood. "You do that. But I have a message for those cronies at Hamilton House, and I want you to give it to them."

"I'm listening."

His father leaned forward, resting his palms on the surface of the desk. "You get on the phone, and you tell them this. Addy and I will never sell 404 Sound. It's our legacy, and we worked too hard to build it up to just hand it off to someone outside the family. And even if we did sell, there's no way in hell we'd ever sell to Hamilton House."

Blaine quipped, "Should I use those exact words, or is it okay if I paraphrase?"

Caleb scowled. "Tell them however you want, smart-ass. Just make sure they get the message, you hear me?"

"I've got it, Dad."

With a huff, Caleb turned on his heel, slung the door open and marched out.

Left alone in his office, Blaine dropped his head against the backrest of his chair and let out an audible groan.

Six

Eden slipped into the recording studio Wednesday around 10:00 a.m. She looked around the empty space, seeing no sign of Blaine or Naiya. She glanced at the time on her phone. *I'm a little early. He should be here soon.* She could remember many slights Blaine had dealt her, but he generally didn't keep her waiting.

She scoffed, shaking her head at the direction of her own thoughts. *What do I know about Blaine, really?* She had only her past interactions with him to go on. She'd thought she knew him well then, which had led to her being blindsided by his betrayal.

She entered the booth, leaving the door ajar so she could hear him when he came in. Hanging her woven purse from the doorknob, she sat down on the stool. In the quiet surroundings, she let her mind wander.

She recalled those days when she was a fresh-faced twentysomething, dreaming of singing superstardom. She, Ainsley and Cambria had pulled many long days and nights in the studio, working on what was supposed to have been their debut album as Swatz Girlz. As a songwriter for the group, Eden had probably put in more hours than her cousin and their good friend.

She'd been spending so much time in the studio with Blaine that, looking back on it now, it seemed only natural that they'd become romantically involved. She remembered the way he watched her when she sang, as if her voice were the most beautiful sound he'd ever heard. She could still feel the warmth that flooded her body whenever he smiled at her, her breath catching when his hand brushed against hers, the way tingles of excitement ran down her spine whenever he kissed her.

She sighed aloud.

Those were the days.

When I was trusting and full of hope.

When I was too young and naive to see what was coming.

The memories of what she'd shared with Blaine seemed so long ago, and simultaneously, it seemed like only yesterday. Her life had changed so much since then. One thing that remained unchanged was her love of music, hip-hop and R & B in particular. It was that love of music that had helped her survive the crushing heartbreak of Blaine's betrayal.

She turned her head to the left, eyeing the instruments occupying one corner of the recording booth. Spying a keyboard sitting on its stand, she scooted the

stool up to it. Turning it on, she set the keyboard to
piano mode and plucked out a few notes. There had
been many times when she'd written songs just this
way—by picking out the basic tune on the keyboard
while working out the lyrics in her head. As the verses
became more solid, she'd start vocalizing to get the ca-
dence just right. It wasn't usually until the second or
third draft that she put the words on paper. Her process
was a bit unorthodox, but it worked well for her.

She ran through the scales a few times, then paused,
her fingers still poised over the keys. The urge to sing
overtook her, and she felt her fingers change position.
Soon, she segued into the opening notes to a classic
tune by Xscape, "My Little Secret." The song, from
their 1998 album *Traces of My Lipstick*, was one of her
favorites of the last two decades. Knowing that group
members Tiny, Tamika, LaTocha and Kandi were fellow Atlanta natives only made her love their work more.

Singing through the opening verse, she could feel
the smile coming over her face. Singing gave her a special kind of joy, a feeling she didn't get from anything
else. Watching Ainsley and Cooper interacting was a
close second, because it touched her heart to see the
genuine love between mother and son. But there was
nothing quite like opening up her mouth and letting
her voice soar.

She was rounding the second chorus when she noticed Blaine standing in the open door to the booth.
Surprised, and a bit embarrassed, she stopped mid-note.

His face filled with earnest admiration, he spoke
into the awkward silence. "Please, Eden. Don't stop."

Heat flared in her chest, and she could feel it rising into her cheeks. "Blaine, I…"

"It's been so long since I've heard you sing." He took a step closer. "I don't want it to be over yet."

Swallowing her nervousness, she picked up where she'd left off. Now that he was in the room, the lyrics, about a secret romance between two people with plenty of baggage, suddenly seemed much more potent.

And personal.

Suddenly, this song, which she often sang in the shower or while driving, simply because she found it catchy, became almost autobiographical. Under the intense, watchful gaze of the man she'd once loved, every word took on new meaning.

She sang the song to the end, then eased her fingertips away from the keys.

Blaine burst into applause. "You've still got it, Eden."

"Thank you," she said, her tone softer than she'd intended. She looked away, reeling from the intimacy of the moment. Having him as a spectator to her impassioned singing felt too familiar, too reminiscent of a time she'd fought hard to forget.

"I'm not just gassing you up, either." His tone quiet, almost reverent, he took a few slow steps until he was right next to her. "I hear singing all day, every day. But I've never, ever come across another voice like yours."

She sucked in a breath, and his rich, woodsy cologne flooded her senses, threatening to undo her. Blowing the breath out, she struggled to find words to articulate her feelings. "I appreciate the compliment, Blaine. I really do. But…"

"But, what?" He watched her intently. "Is something wrong?"

She tucked in her bottom lip. *How can I tell him that being this close to him ruins my concentration? That I can't focus on my work because all I want to do is climb him like a tree?*

"Eden?"

"I'm fine." She shifted on the stool, angling her face away from him in hopes that she might regain some of her faculties. His physical size, combined with his overt masculine energy, seemed to fill the space around her, making the booth feel even smaller than it actually was.

He reached out, his fingertips brushing lightly over her bare shoulder. "Are you sure?"

She trembled, reacting to the tingling sensation brought on by his electric touch. For a moment, she wanted him to continue, wanted to feel his kiss. Soon, though, common sense took over, and she shook her head. "Yes, Blaine. I'm positive."

Blaine took a step back from Eden, concerned he might be invading her space. Even though she insisted she was fine, he sensed the discomfort rolling off her. Clearing his throat, he said, "Feel free to speak honestly with me, Eden. We've known each other too long to be dishonest with each other."

"If I had something to say, trust me, I'd say it." She tossed the words over her shoulder, still not facing him.

He sighed. "Well, I do have something to say." He jammed his hands into his pockets, trying to get the words to line up in his mind. She looked so beautiful today, in a sunny yellow sleeveless blouse and a pair of wide-legged white linen pants that hugged her hips like he used to when they were making love. "I've... missed you."

She glanced over her shoulder at him, her eyes wide.

He cleared his throat, trying to cover what had been too honest an admission. "I meant... I've missed working with you." He could feel his blood warming. No other woman had ever left him so discombobulated.

She did a slow turn on the stool, facing him again. Her hair, tied back in a low ponytail, highlighted the beauty of her bronze-skinned face. Her expression held a mixture of surprise and annoyance. "Oh, really? You've missed working with me, but you never called on me to write for you before now."

He missed more than just working with her, but something told him now wasn't the time to mention that. "Just like your voice, your writing talents are unique, special. Up until now, I haven't had an artist I felt could carry what you bring to the table."

"Laying it on pretty thick, huh?" She chuckled, shaking her head. "If you say so."

"It's true." And it was, partially, at least. He did think Naiya was perfectly suited to Eden's songwriting style. But he'd also stayed away from Eden because she'd made it clear she didn't want him around. After he'd been forced to cut her and Ainsley from his roster, things had soured between them in a major way. Both their personal and professional relationship had been flushed down the toilet that day, and he didn't know if they'd ever get back to a good place. Still, part of him wanted to try.

"Why are you staring at me, Blaine?" A curious half smile came over her face.

He sensed her goading him. Still, he decided to take a serious tack. "Eden, you do realize I didn't have a choice, right? I had to do what I did."

"Oh, boy." She shook her head. "Here we go."

"Honestly. I had a lot of faith in Swatz Girlz as a group. But I had to make sure I had funding to make my business successful."

She laughed, slapping her thigh. "Do you realize you said the same thing back then? It's the same old line about how you didn't have a choice. But the thing is, you did. It's *your* business, Blaine. You always have a choice." She fixed him with a look, her eyes slightly narrowed. "You chose."

That's easy for her to say. She could never understand what it was like to be him. People tended to assume that because of his family's money, his whole life had been some sort of leisurely stroll through the garden. Nothing could be further from the truth. "Come on, Eden. You're not being fair here."

She snorted. "I think it's a very fair judgment. You did what was best for you, I get that. But you have to admit to not giving much thought to what would happen to us. You know, you and me? The relationship we were building? Did you give any thought at all to the future we could have had?"

He shoved his hands into the pockets of his jeans.

"Why can't you see things for what they are? Why do you insist on thinking the worst of me?"

She rolled her eyes. "I can only go by what you've shown me. You'll have to excuse me for not seeing you as some kind of saint."

He groaned. "I never claimed to be a saint, but..." He stopped mid-sentence.

Their gazes locked, and silence fell.

Seeing the fire dancing in her dark eyes made his body temperature rise. All he wanted was to hold her, to possess her as he once had. In an instant, his anger melted away, replaced by a consuming desire to pull her into his arms. What was it about this woman that had him vacillating between wanting to verbally spar with her and wanting to ravish her? Before he could stop himself, he grasped her hand.

"Blaine?" Her lips were slightly parted, begging to be kissed.

Giving her a gentle tug, he growled, "Stand up."

She did as he asked. "Why?"

"So, I don't have to kneel to do this." He grazed his fingertips along her jawline.

Her eyes closed briefly, then popped open again. "If you kiss me, I'll box your ears."

"You can't even reach my ears," he teased.

"I'll get a step stool."

"If you do, I'll take my lumps like a man." He eased the tip of his index finger over her lips. "Just let me have this one kiss."

A soft chuckle escaped her throat. "Damn it, Blaine."

She angled her face up, pressing her lips together in a soft pucker.

Moments later, he kissed her. The contact, heady and all too fleeting, sent sparks of desire dancing down his spine like electricity moving along a fallen power line. Her lips were soft and yielding, just as he remembered them. After a few more soft brushes, he deepened the kiss. Sweeping his tongue over her lower lip, he thrilled when she opened her mouth for him. As he slipped his tongue inside, a soft moan escaped her throat, and he nearly came undone. He knew that if they continued, he'd be laying her down on the sofa and taking her until she cried out his name. Reluctantly, he eased away.

"You're made of temptation, Eden Voss."

She placed her fingertips against her lips. Her eyes were glazed with desire, but as always, she deflected with her trademark humor. "I should have made you kneel."

Now it was his turn to chuckle. "Maybe I'll kneel for you later."

"Hey, guys."

A third voice entered the conversation, and he turned toward the sound.

Naiya had appeared in the doorway. She leaned against the doorframe, glancing back and forth between them. "Sorry, am I interrupting something?"

Blaine shook his head, tearing his gaze away from Eden. "No. We're just talking shop." He kept his tone even, not wanting to reveal the delicious tension of the preceding moments. "So, Naiya, how are you feeling about the single so far?"

"It's great. I'm ready to move forward with the process."

"Ready enough to lay down some reference vocals on your single?" he asked.

Naiya smiled, her excitement apparent. "Let's do it."

He looked her way again. "Eden, you can stay in the booth with Naiya and give her delivery tips as we go along, okay?" He tried to direct his thoughts back to business, but it was all he could do to stand up straight after how hard she'd made him. She glanced down, a ghost of a smile crossing her face.

She nodded. "Sure thing."

She knows. He thought about the frigid snowfall from his last winter vacation in the Colorado mountains until his ardor finally calmed enough for him to walk.

He left the booth, letting the door close behind him. Moments later, he was at the soundboard. Giving them a thumbs-up through the glass partition, he put on his headphones and started the playback of the track.

While he bobbed his head along with the music, he did his best to shake off the memory of Eden's kiss. But just like any great composition, the melody of her was impossible to shake.

Seven

Friday morning, Eden stifled a yawn as she entered the Bodacious Bean. The air-conditioned interior provided immediate relief from the sticky August air, and she sighed as soon as the door shut behind her. The combination of the oppressive humidity, high temperature and a lack of quality sleep the night before had left her feeling like a zombie, and she desperately needed a caffeine pick-me-up.

She'd spent the better part of the night tossing and turning, unable to sleep. And when she had finally drifted off, Blaine and his magnificent kisses were waiting for her in dreamland. She just couldn't seem to shake her desire for him. She craved his touch the way flowers craved sunlight.

Ponying up to the counter, she greeted the barista

and ordered an iced coffee with two shots of espresso. Once she had the coffee and a blueberry muffin in hand, she slunk to a table near the back. As she sucked down the first sip of her drink, her phone buzzed. Picking it up, she glanced at the screen before answering. "Hey, Ainsley. What's up?"

"What's up with you? You barely said two words to me last night when you came in, and then you bounced this morning before I even got up."

She stifled another yawn. "Sorry, girl. I was exhausted."

"You sound like you're still tired. What's going on with you? Didn't you sleep last night?"

She drank a bit more coffee before answering. "Not as well as I would have liked."

"Mmm-hmm."

She rolled her eyes even though she knew her cousin couldn't see it. "Mmm-hmm, what?"

"There's something you're not telling me, Eden. I just know it." Ainsley's tone dripped with suspicion.

"Dang, Ainsley. You're always grilling me. Even my mama didn't get in my business as you do."

"Well, my mama did. I'm just picking up where she left off."

Shaking her head at how much Ainsley reminded her of Aunt Mimi, she sighed. "Fine. I got to the studio a little early Wednesday, so I sat down to the keyboard… Anyway, Blaine walked in on me playing and singing."

"Were you singing that Xscape song? The one you're always belting out around the house?"

She laughed. "Yes, I was. Anyway, it's been so long

since I got to play and sing like that. And it really reminded me how much I miss singing professionally..."

Ainsley interjected. "Boo, we both know you miss singing. But it ain't never been serious enough to keep you up at night. So why don't you stop beating around the bush and tell me the real tea, okay?"

Yikes. She chewed on the plastic straw. "Ainsley, you're killing me."

"Then let's make it quick. Or would you rather drag it out and lengthen your suffering?"

Annoyed as she was, she couldn't help laughing at her cousin. "Okay. Blaine started talking about how he missed working with me, and I fussed at him a little."

"So, you couldn't sleep because y'all argued?"

"No, that's not it. And I wouldn't call it an argument, it was more of a heated discussion. Even though we were having a pretty heavy conversation, somehow, he...ended up kissing me." Retelling the tale to her cousin forced her to relive those torrid moments wrapped in his arms. She could still smell his cologne, still feel the strength of his arms enfolding her...

"I knew it!"

She dropped the phone on the table. Picking it up a moment later, she groused, "Can you not shout in my ear? It's way too early for these shenanigans."

"I'm not gonna say I told you so."

"You literally just did."

Ainsley laughed. "Well, I'm not gonna say it twice. Anyway, I knew that as soon as y'all got in that studio together, the sparks would start flying."

"Don't you have something to be doing right now?"

"I'm in the kitchen making Cooper some breakfast."

"Good. Well, I'll let you go so you can focus on cooking before you burn the house down. We're already paying for the roof, and I don't need any more mishaps."

"But…"

She hung up on her cousin, laying her phone face down on the table. Part of the reason she'd left so early was so she could get her coffee and have it quietly, giving the caffeine time to do its magic before she had to be at the studio. No way was she about to give up that peaceful start to her day to play a game of twenty-one questions with her well-meaning but nosy cousin. She was still processing what had transpired between her and Blaine and discussing it with Ainsley certainly wasn't helping her achieve clarity.

After draining the contents of her cup, she popped off the lid and headed back to the counter for a refill. Just as she got her filled cup back, the bell above the door sounded and she turned.

Blaine walked in.

She nearly dropped her coffee. Snapping the lid back on, she swallowed. *It's too early for anybody to be looking that damn good.*

True to his usual style, he wore a pair of distressed black jeans, black leather sneakers and a black T-shirt bearing the Against the Grain logo in metallic silver. The signature large sunglasses once again obscured his eyes, and his locs were tied in a haphazard knot atop his head. His lips tilted into a smile when he saw her. "Morning, Eden."

"Good morning." Her voice squeaked out, barely above a whisper.

"You've…got a little something…" He gestured, pointing toward her face. "You know, right around your mouth."

She brushed away the crumbs of blueberry muffin clinging there, then blew out a breath. "Ever had the muffins here? They're pretty great."

"Yeah, they are." He advanced toward the counter. "You okay?"

She ran her free hand over her hair, hoping it resembled something like a style. She spoke again, a bit louder this time. "Yes, I'm fine. I'm just low on caffeine."

"Me, too. But at least you came to the right place."

She eased back toward her table, and part of her hoped that he'd get his drink to go, and that would be the end of their interaction, at least until she made it to the studio. She sat down, pretending to scroll through her phone while taking surreptitious glances in his direction.

When she saw him walking toward her, coffee in hand, she knew her hopes of him leaving her to finish her coffee alone had been dashed on the jagged rocks of reality. Drawing a breath, she braced for his entry into her personal bubble.

He paused near the empty chair across the table from her. "Mind if I sit with you for a bit?"

While this wasn't what she'd planned, she could think of far worse company to be in. With a soft smile, she said, "Have a seat."

"Thanks." He set his paper cup down on the table as he eased into the seat.

Silence fell between them for a moment, and she tried not to look at his lips. She failed, and the memory of his kiss rose to the surface. Looking at him only made her remember the delicious pressure of his lips against hers. She took another sip of her drink, noting the way he rubbed the back of his neck. With his eyes still hidden behind the dark lenses, she couldn't fully read his mood. "Is there something you want to talk about?" She realized too late that the question had been too open-ended, but since she couldn't take it back, she just hoped for the best.

He cleared his throat. "There is, actually. I was wondering if there's anything we could do to speed up the process of completing Naiya's album."

She picked up on something in his voice, something she wasn't used to hearing from the confident label head. *Is he nervous about something? Is it because he kissed me, or is it business-related?* "I've already started drafting the second song, if that's what you mean."

"No. I mean, can we speed up the timeline for the project as a whole? I'd really like to get ten solid tracks done in less than a month, if possible."

She contemplated his words for a moment. While she was glad he hadn't taken her question as an invitation to discuss kissing, she couldn't help feeling curious about his sudden rush to finish Naiya's album. "I suppose I could. However, debut albums can be tricky, and I want to do my best work for her."

"I understand, and trust me, I appreciate that. But I'm on a bit of a time crunch, though I'd rather not discuss why."

She wasn't thrilled that he seemed to be hiding something from her, but this was Blaine Woodson, after all. "I think it might help my process if I could see her perform live. Just to get a better feel for her style and how she interacts with a crowd."

He brightened, clapped his hands together. "Great! Then you can come with me to her open mic show at the Bass Line Lounge tomorrow night."

She studied his face, trying to ascertain his intent. "Are you asking me on a date, Blaine?"

He chuckled. "No. It's not a date. It's business. I'm simply giving you what you say will help your process."

"Good. So that means there won't be any flirting, or kissing…"

He chuckled again, a deep, rumbling sound that seemed to reverberate through his broad chest. "Don't worry. I won't kiss you again until you ask me to."

She swallowed hard. It was impossible to miss the teasing in his tone, yet she knew he meant what he said. She also knew that the odds were pretty good that she would cave and ask for his kisses again…she just wasn't going to tell him that now.

She rolled her eyes. "Awesome. That means it will never happen again."

That afternoon, Blaine retreated to his office while Naiya and Eden worked in the booth. He'd left Trevor, his engineer, to operate the soundboard while he handled some of the tasks he'd let pile up on his desk over the last few weeks. He didn't relish this mundane part of the job, but after he delegated as much as he could to Leanna, his assistant, he had no choice but to complete the rest.

He slid aside a small stack of completed paperwork and set his pen down, flexing his fingers to relieve some of the stiffness in his joints. With the papers tucked away in a folder, he dropped his head back against the headrest of his executive chair. His gaze was on the ceiling, but his mind was on the morning encounter he'd had with Eden.

He hadn't been expecting to run into her at the coffee shop but seeing her had given his day an instant lift. Since his mind had been on his problems with Hamilton House, he hadn't been able to take the conversation in the direction he'd have wanted. He'd wanted to talk about kissing her, specifically, about how soon he could kiss her again. The memory of her soft, yielding lips and the way her skin felt beneath his fingertips made him yearn for more.

Instead, he'd steered the conversation to work. He'd asked her to work harder, faster, to produce the lyrics for Naiya's album. It wasn't ideal, but he didn't have much of a choice. *If I want to remain competitive, keep Against the Grain on the cutting edge, and most of all, keep my main source of funding, I've got to level up.*

He didn't want to put pressure on her, professionally or personally. But he wanted Eden, in all the ways a man could want a woman. And though she would probably rather get a root canal than admit to it, she wanted him, too. So, he'd wait. Patience had never been a strength of his, so he knew it wouldn't be easy.

The struggle is real. But she's absolutely worth it.

His stream of thought was interrupted by the intercom chime on his desk phone.

Leanna's voice came over the speaker. "Blaine, Pierce Hamilton is here."

He felt his brow crinkle with annoyance. He'd only had a few interactions in the past with Pierce, the son of reclusive company owner, the widowed Everly Hamilton. None of them had been particularly positive. Pierce came across as an arrogant, entitled, self-absorbed man who'd gladly step on someone's throat to get his own way. "I don't want to deal with him right now...tell him I'm unavailable."

"I told him that...unfortunately he's already on his way down the..."

Before Leanna could complete the sentence, Blaine's office door swung open. Pierce strode in, his fingertips attached to the lapels of his expensive sports jacket as if he feared the jacket might fly away if he didn't hold on to it. "Greetings, Blake."

"It's *Blaine*." He emphasized the word through his tightly set teeth. Pierce never seemed to get his name right, and while he wasn't surprised, he still found it grating.

"Oh, yes, of course." Pierce took a seat in the guest chair across from him, settling in as if he planned to stay for a while. "So, tell me. How are you? How have things been going?" He laced his fingers together, watching Blaine as if awaiting his answer with great anticipation.

Blaine responded with an icy half smile. "I'm fine, thanks for asking. But I'm sure this isn't a social call." He leaned back in his chair. "So, what can I do for you, Mr. Hamilton?"

He waved his hand. "Pshaw. Mr. Hamilton was my father, God rest his soul. Call me Pierce."

I'd call him an asshole, but I'm sure that wouldn't fly. "If you insist. So, what motivated this little impromptu visit?"

Pierce leaned to the right, resting his chin in the crook between his thumb and index finger. "Quite frankly, I'm surprised you don't know. I hear our label liaison is a real chatterbox."

Blaine felt the tightness build at the base of his spine, crawling up his back like a spider. *I can see where this conversation is headed. No need to put all my cards on the table, though.* "I'm not big on gossip. So why don't you just tell me?"

"We've been talking about expanding the Hamilton House empire." Pierce offered a sly smile that showed off the diamond set in his upper left incisor. "We're looking at creative ways to be the biggest, most comprehensive music production company in the American South…and then, in the whole country."

Blaine kept his tone even, training his expression to remain flat. "Sounds like you've got big dreams."

"You're right. But it's not just me. Mother and my dear sister London are also on board with this vision for the future."

"This all sounds very exciting, Pete."

His eyes flashed. "It's *Pierce*."

"Of course. My apologies." It pleased him to give the man a taste of his own medicine. Still, this back-and-forth banter had started to lose its luster. "I'm still not seeing how this relates to me."

The flash of anger disappeared, replaced by a smug grin. "We've got our eyes on 404 Sound. It's the perfect addition to the brand, and it would give us control of one of the most state-of-the-art studios in this part of the country."

His shoulders stiffened as the spiderlike legs of tension spread. So it was true. "That seems to have more to do with my parents than it does with me. As you know, I'm not affiliated with 404."

Pierce chuckled. "Oh, it has more to do with you than you think. Because if we're going to buy out 404, we'll need an infusion of capital. Mother hates to come out of pocket on these things if it can be avoided." He leaned forward in his chair, his gaze focused squarely on Blaine's face. "And the best way to get that capital, at least as far as I can see, is to stop funding Against the Grain. That way, we can easily redirect those funds to this new endeavor." He scratched his chin. "I suppose we'd hold on to your label if your performance improved dramatically...but I don't really see that happening."

The tenuous hold Blaine had over his expression slipped. Pierce must have seen the change because he immediately straightened in his seat, putting more distance between them. "It's really strange that you came by, Pierce. Because my father was here a few days ago.

Apparently, he'd already heard about this little buyout plan, and he left a message for me to convey to Hamilton House."

Pierce laced his fingers together. "I'd love to hear it." His tone held both challenge and thinly veiled contempt.

Blaine stood, towering over Pierce. "I'll paraphrase for you. My parents aren't selling 404. And even if they did, they'd never sell it to the likes of you." He gestured to the door. "Now if you'll excuse me, I need to get back to work. Have yourself a great day."

Pierce stood quickly, nearly toppling the guest chair in the process. "We'll see each other again, Woodson." He slid his gaze upward since Blaine towered over him by a good five inches.

"I'm sure we will." He continued to gesture to the door.

Pierce narrowed his eyes but said nothing. Moments later, with his fingertips locked on his lapels again, he strode out.

Eight

Saturday night, Eden handed her ticket to the gargantuan bouncer. Once he'd nodded his approval, she entered the dimly lit Bass Line Lounge. The club, spacious and open, had foregone the typical setup of crowding the floor with a lot of tables. There was a glossy marble bar that occupied the wall directly in front of her, the gleaming mirrored shelves stocked with liquor of every variety. Cozy booths lined the east and west walls, providing seating as well as a modicum of privacy for those who desired it. Centering the space was a stage, with the DJ spinning records on an elevated platform. Just below the booth were drums, a keyboard and speakers.

Circling past the stage and to her right, she glanced around the place. *I'll head to the bar. That way he won't have to search for me when he comes in.*

Maybe Blaine was already in the building. She imagined him somewhere backstage, giving Naiya a pep talk as she prepared to go onstage. What kinds of things would he say to the talented young singer? She slid onto an empty barstool, feeling her jaw tense as she followed that line of thinking. Would he smile at her? Remind her of her talent? Praise her? *Is he telling her all the things he used to say to me?*

"Miss?"

The voice dragged her out of her own head and back to reality. Looking up, she saw the bartender standing nearby. He slid her a cocktail napkin. "Anything to drink?"

"Just a ginger ale for now, thanks."

He moved away to get her drink, and she released a quiet sigh. Thinking about those days always made her a little melancholy, so she avoided it most of the time. Like most of her recollections, these had a soundtrack. J. Cole, Kendrick Lamar, 2 Chainz. Miguel's impassioned crooning accompanying Wale's rhymes, Elle Varner craving a little more of that good conversation.

Swept up in the moment, the floodgates opened, and she let herself be carried away by the deluge of memories.

Those nights in the studio, the booth dimly lit. His hands working the controls at the soundboard while she sat on a stool by the microphone, pouring her heart out in song. Sitting next to him, their hips barely touching, while they bopped their heads to the playback. He'd smelled of expensive cologne, the light watery scent blending with the jasmine incense she still burned when she sat down to write.

The bartender set her ginger ale down, jarring her out of her thoughts, and she thanked him as he moved away with a smile. Sipping from the glass, she turned on her stool.

Blaine stood there, less than two feet away. He wore a metallic gray button-down shirt dotted with dark blue feathers, the top two buttons left open. A black sport coat, slacks and polished loafers completed his ensemble.

His locs hung down around his shoulders, unbound. Their gazes met, and the moment that wicked smile tipped his full lips, something inside her clenched, then unfurled.

The glass slipped from her hand, clattering to the carpeted floor with a clanking thud. Only the splash of ice-cold liquid hitting her bare thigh made her draw her eyes away from Blaine's blinding fineness.

Entering her space, he stooped to pick up the glass and set it on the bar. "You okay, Eden?"

She nodded, unable to speak for the moment.

"You sure?" He took a small step back, his gaze appreciative as it swept over her body. "Because you certainly look fantastic."

Her cheeks warmed, and she cleared her throat. "I'm fine, Blaine. And thanks for the compliment."

He sat down on the stool to her right. "Been here long?"

Just long enough to have impure thoughts about you... She shook her head. "Just a few minutes."

"Do you wanna stay at the bar? Because I reserved us a prime booth so we can get a good view of the show." His eyes connected with hers. "And...so we can talk."

She swallowed, her throat dry. "We can go to the booth. Just let me replace this drink." Gesturing for the bartender, she got a new ginger ale, then followed Blaine to the booth.

As he'd promised, their position gave them a great view of the stage. The intimacy of the booth, with its high backed, U-shaped bench upholstered in black leather, made him seem even bigger than his usual tall, broad-shouldered self. He eased close to her toward the center of the bench but left a respectable space between them. With any other man, she'd have considered his nearness an imposition on her personal space. But since this was Blaine Woodson, she scooted nearer to him, stopping when his muscular thigh brushed against hers.

"This is cozy," he remarked with a wink. While watching her, he tossed his arm casually around her shoulder, as if waiting to see if she'd move away.

She didn't. The voice of logic, the one that told her she was treading on thin ice by getting this close to him, was increasingly drowned out by another, more assertive voice. The one that had awakened the moment she'd entered his office and seen him for the first time in seven years.

This man is too gorgeous for you to be fronting like you don't want him. She almost chuckled aloud, because it sounded like something Ainsley would have said.

"What's on your mind over there, Eden?"

She smiled, but before she could open her mouth to

answer, the house lights were turned out, signaling the start of the show. A short Black man in a cherry-red suit stepped into the spotlight on stage, bowing graciously at the applause that met him.

"Welcome, y'all, to the Bass Line Lounge's New Artist Showcase." He paused for a second wave of applause. "For those of you that don't know me, I'm Ray Price, owner of this fine establishment. Tonight, we're proud to welcome two upcoming acts from right here in the ATL. First up, singer Naiya B. Come on up, Miss Naiya." He gestured to the area just to the left of the stage.

Eden watched as Naiya climbed the two metal steps up to the stage. After exchanging a hug with Ray as he exited, she approached the stool and the microphone stand, offering a curtsy in response to the cheers in the room. She wore a strapless black one-piece pantsuit with wide legs. An ankle-length white floral kimono covered her arms, the fabric billowing around her as she moved. Her mass of curls cascaded around her shoulders, and huge silver hoop earrings peeked out from among the ringlets. An acoustic guitar, mounted on a tan leather strap, hung on her back.

"Good evening, y'all. I want to thank Ray and Neil for having me tonight. My name is Naiya B." She paused for another smattering of hoots and hollers. "Some of you may know me from the videos I've posted on Beyoncé's internet."

Laughs sounded throughout the room, and Eden found herself chuckling as well.

Naiya sat down on the edge of the stool, swinging the

guitar around to the front. "What you might not know is that I'm currently in the studio, recording my very first album. I'm excited to share a little something from that project with you later on tonight." She plucked a few notes on the guitar. "But before we get into that, let's start out with a classic, shall we?" She played a few more notes, segueing into an emphatic cover of Lauryn Hill's hit "The Sweetest Thing."

I love this song. Eden found herself swaying in her seat, her body moving of its own accord. A quintessential late-nineties ballad, the song spoke of the bittersweet memory of young love, bursting with hope and passion, but finally falling victim to the harshness of reality. Naiya's cover paid homage to Hill's original without being a direct imitation and showcased the young singer's incredible vocal range.

By the time Naiya hit the soaring notes of the vamp, Eden's hand went to her chest. "She's magical." Turning toward Blaine, she found him staring at her. The intensity of his gaze shook her to the core.

He reached out, gently cupped his hand around her chin. "I know. I'm very familiar with magic."

Blaine stared into Eden's dark eyes, reading the wonder they displayed. He'd struggled to hold back from touching her, and now that her silken face rested on his hand, he knew he wanted to do so much more. That decision wasn't his to make, but he'd plead his case as earnestly as he knew how.

She looks so beautiful tonight.

Dressed in that hot little one-shouldered white minidress, paired with metallic gold high-heeled sandals, she was a stunner. No other woman in the club could hold a candle to her. And while his main purpose in being here tonight was to support his newest artist, he had a difficult time taking his eyes off his gorgeous companion.

"Blaine." She whispered his name.

Still cupping her chin, he said, "Yes?"

"People are staring at us."

He didn't bother to verify what she'd said, because it didn't matter to him who saw them. "I don't care. But if I'm making you uncomfortable..."

"It's not that." Her cheeks were warm and slightly reddened. "It's just... I'm trying to focus on Naiya's performance. That's why I'm here, remember?"

He released her, nodding. "Of course." Though parts of him were bereft at the loss of contact between his hand and her scented skin, he knew she was right. He turned his gaze back to the stage.

She shifted on the bench. "That doesn't mean we can't continue this later, after the show."

He glanced her way, and she gave him the sauciest little wink. His heart skipped a beat. *Is she finally softening up?*

Grinning, he looked again toward Naiya, illuminated by the spotlight. Applause filled the space as she ended the song. "Thank you so much. Next, I've got another familiar tune some of you might know." Two black-clad female background singers eased into position behind her, their microphone stands flanking Naiya's stool. She strummed her fingers over the strings again, this time easing into India.Arie's "Steady Love."

Eden watched, her expression conveying her awe. "Look how easily she segues between eras. She's so fluid, so versatile." She leaned forward, tenting her fingers as her elbows rested on the table. "That's definitely going to help with the songwriting for her album."

"She's really in her element up there, isn't she?"

She nodded. "Yes, she's a dynamic performer. But what I'm really getting is a good sense of her range as a singer. She's already given me her journal, so I know what's in her heart. Seeing her on stage like this will help me translate her thoughts and feelings into lyrics more effectively."

"Great. I'm glad this is helpful for you." He scratched his chin, wondering what kind of things the two women would come up with once they returned to the studio. He was anxious to hear the outcome, and not just because of the added pressure placed on him by recent happenings at Hamilton House. He only took on artists if he felt fully invested in developing their careers, so he truly wanted to see Naiya showcase her vocal prowess on her debut project.

He did his best to pay attention for the rest of Naiya's forty-five-minute set, and he caught most of it. But sitting so close to Eden had his mind slowed and throwed, as if DJ Screw himself were inside his head, working the crossfader back and forth. He found that focusing on anything other than her brown-skinned beauty required a hell of a lot of effort.

"So it's time for my last song, folks." Naiya leaned into the microphone, her voice rising over the quiet din of conversation and clinking glasses. "It's the first single from my upcoming album *Capitol View Soul*..." She paused, smiling out at the audience as a cheer went up at the mention of her neighborhood. "Oh, I see y'all. We in the building? Capitol View, stand up!" A few more hoots and hollers followed her acknowledgment. When the room quieted, she spoke again. "This song is called 'The Way It Was,' and I hope y'all like it."

The DJ dropped the needle, and Naiya set her guitar and stool aside, standing at the microphone. While her background singers provided harmonious accompaniment, she belted out the song, her love letter to the neighborhood that had nurtured her. She and her singers even threw in a few simple, choreographed steps, upping the entertainment value. Folks clapped along, and Blaine felt his foot tapping beneath the table. Looking around the room, he noted the bobbing heads, the pumping fists.

People are feeling the vibe. This is definitely a good sign.

By the time Naiya hit the song's soaring final note, most of the crowd was on its feet. A rousing round of cheers and applause shook the club as Naiya and the two singers took their bows. Blowing kisses to her audience of new fans, she jogged out of the spotlight and off stage.

Blaine tapped Eden on the shoulder. "Come on, let's go congratulate our superstar." He slid out of the booth, then held out his hand to help her to her feet.

She slipped her hand into his, smiling. That familiar electric charge snaked up her arm in response to his touch, and she relished the sensation. Slinging her purse strap over her bare shoulder, she maintained the contact as they navigated through the crowd toward the stage area.

They found Naiya standing among a tangle of enthusiastic admirers. Blaine stood back, watching as people jockeyed for selfies with the young singer or asked her to sign various items. Then he spoke with his artist briefly, offering his congratulations on a great performance. Naiya then left to celebrate her accomplishment with a few friends. As soon as she was gone, Blaine turned back to Eden. "Now. About what you said earlier…"

Her expression turned coy. "I'm not sure what you're referring to, Blaine."

He feigned distress. "Come on, Eden. What do I have to do to get you to spend some time with me? You want me to grovel? Get down on my knees and beg like Jodeci?" He held his hands up. "What's a brotha gotta do to get on your good side, girl?"

She laughed, shaking her head. "You're crazy, you know that?"

"Yes. I also know that most of the reason I'm acting this way is you." He moved a bit closer to her. "So what do you say? Give me a shot?"

She sighed, but a slight smile tipped her glossy lips. "Let's go for a walk."

He frowned, confused. "Now?" It was after ten on a Saturday night, after all.

She nodded. "Yes. Take me to Piedmont Park." She folded her arms over her chest.

He cocked his brow. "Piedmont Park, eh? I know you remember what happened the last time we were there."

"How can I forget when you keep bringing it up?"

He chuckled. "Don't act like you don't like it."

She rolled her eyes in an exaggerated fashion. "Whatever, Blaine. Do you want to go, or not? Unless you have something else you'd rather be doing right now?" He eased closer to her, dragging his fingertip over the satin line of her jaw. Then he leaned close to her ear, his voice low as he spoke. "I can assure you, the only thing I want to be doing right now is you."

She gave him a wicked smile. "Then let's go."

Nine

A half hour later, with the moon sitting low in the sky, Eden walked hand in hand with Blaine through the Twelfth Street Gate at Piedmont Park. She'd brought her trusty blue twill blanket from the trunk of her car, and had it slung over her bare shoulder. The night had given way to a cooler, breezier atmosphere, a welcome respite from the day's oppressive heat and humidity.

There weren't many people out this time of night, save a few folks walking their dogs or taking an evening jog. The subtle song of crickets, grasshoppers and frogs mingled with the whir of passing traffic whizzing around Midtown.

"It's so nice outside," she remarked as they strolled down the concrete path. The city light shimmering beyond the treetops only added to the beauty of the night.

This was the city she'd grown up in, the place she loved. And while some might crave the wide-open spaces of the plains or the sandy beaches of the coast, she loved her hometown, the crown jewel of the southeast.

"It is." Blaine squeezed her hand. "Company's not bad, either."

She winked as they passed the I-shaped structure of the Ladies Waiting Room.

"Mind telling me why you insisted on coming here?" He eyed her curiously.

She tugged him along by the hand, around the circular path leading to the Clara Meer Dock. When they came to a stop, she pointed. "This is why I wanted to come here."

He looked out, his eyes scanning the dark, glassy surface of Lake Clara Meer. "I'm guessing you come here often?"

She nodded. "This is my thinking spot. Whenever I'm working on lyrics and I can't quite get it right, I come here. I spread my blanket out on the grass, sit down with my notepad and work it out."

He looked at her skeptically. "So, did we come here to work?"

"Nah." She shook her head. "It's Saturday night, after all. I brought you here to talk."

He frowned. "I'm still confused."

She started walking over to the grassy patch overlooking the water and the dock and spread out the blanket there. "Something about this place always seems to bring me clarity. It's a little slice of heaven, right in the middle of the city. It's bound to inspire some pretty deep conversation between us." She sat down, careful not to let her dress ride up till heaven and earth were filled with her glory. Then she patted the empty spot next to her.

He hesitated, standing there on the concrete path, looking a bit baffled.

"You scared, Blaine?" She faked a pout, sticking her lip out as she teased him. "Of little old me?"

He rolled his eyes, but his smile was evident as he joined her on the blanket. "You're too much, Eden."

"So, we're basically alone now." *Or at least as close to alone as we're gonna get without me crawling into your lap.* She watched him, taking in his moon-dappled handsomeness. The dim lighting seemed to enhance his features, especially the golden flecks in his dark eyes. He was temptation in the flesh; her body craved him even though her mind knew better than to get lost in him again. The question was, how much longer would she be able to lead with logic? "What do you want to talk about?"

He cleared his throat. "If I'm being honest…"

"Please do," she encouraged.

"I want to talk about kissing you again." His deep baritone had each word dripping with sensual energy.

Warmth raced through her body, and she felt it pool in her cheeks, her chest and a bit farther south. "Blaine." She meant it as chastisement, but it came out sounding far sultrier than she'd intended.

He shrugged. "Can't blame a brotha for shooting his shot."

"I guess not." She chuckled, from both amusement

and nerves. "I don't know if we should lead with talking about kissing, though."

"Why not?" He gave her a wicked look. "Did you enjoy the kiss?"

She swallowed and needing a respite from the intensity of his gaze, she looked down at her lap. Her dress had crept up her to mid-thigh, so she tugged the end a bit. "I'd be lying if I said I didn't enjoy it. But that's beside the point."

"If you say so."

She shook her head. *Same old Blaine. Always charming, never reflective.* "There's too much in our past that you're not considering, Blaine. We can't just ignore our history."

"Who said I'm ignoring it?" He traced a finger along her lower leg, trailing from her knee to the top of her sandal-encased foot. "What I know about you, our 'history' as you call it, is precisely why I want you."

She drew a deep breath. Was he misremembering? Or was he really so clueless that he didn't understand where she was coming from? "You know your decision to cut Ainsley and me from the group effectively ended both of our singing careers, right? Not to mention how much it hurt me personally. You have to realize the impact of that."

He tilted his head to the side. "We talked about this, Eden. Do I have to remind you again that my hands were tied?"

Now he was just being obtuse. "You keep saying that as if you truly had no other options. I never understood why you were so determined to do things on your own anyway. Why couldn't you have just joined up with your family at 404?"

"Dad and I were…not on good terms. He wasn't exactly pleased when I left the family business to strike out on my own, and his disappointment has only grown since then."

"You should have tried to repair the relationship. Who knows? Maybe he would have helped you achieve your vision for the group."

"I doubt it. We were barely speaking then, and not much has changed."

Her expression earnest, she said, "Family should always come first, Blaine. You should have reached out to him. If he's holding on to anger, you should try to make up with him."

His brow creased into a frown, and he withdrew his touch. "You wouldn't understand. It's more complex than it seems on the surface."

He's right. I wouldn't understand. His family is still intact. My father walked out on my mother before I took my first steps, and now my mother is gone. Ainsley and Cooper are the only family I have left.

She sighed. "I didn't bring you out here to argue. It goes against everything I love about this place. Let's just agree to disagree for now."

"Can we still kiss? You know…while we're disagreeing and all?" A glimmer of hope shone in his eyes.

She pursed her lips. "Honestly, Blaine…" The thought of kissing him appealed to her like a decadent dessert, but risking her heart again wasn't something she wanted to do.

"Listen. What happened in the past isn't nearly as important as what's happening right now." He reached out, enfolded her hand inside his own. "And what's happening now is that I'm attracted to you, Eden Voss. If you truly feel I wronged you in the past, then please, give me a shot at making it up to you. That's why I brought you on for Naiya's project."

"So, you hired me to pay penance for your actions in the past?"

"Only partly." He held her gaze, hoping she could see his sincerity. "I also believe in your talent. The label wasn't thrilled about my plan to bring you on. But I have absolute faith in you."

It's a start...that's probably the best I'm going to get out of him for now. She'd held on to her resentment like a favorite accessory for so many years. But ever since he'd been back in her life, the part of her that still cared for him, still found him irresistible, threatened to snatch that bitterness away.

"You got quiet," he said, his voice just above a whisper. "What's on your mind?"

She drew a shaky inhale, then let the words fall out. "I want to kiss you again, Blaine. So, help me, I know it's a terrible idea. But I..."

He silenced her by dragging her close and pressing his lips against hers.

A soft moan escaped her mouth, flowing into his, and he deepened the kiss in response. Leaning into him, she opened her mouth. Their tongues mated and played, while his hands roved over the sensitive flesh of her shoulders, her arms, her thighs. His hot mouth and his skilled caress fired her blood. She could feel her heart thumping, hard and fast, while the thrill of his touch reverberated through her body like sound waves.

Blaine held Eden's soft body close to his, drawing out the kiss for as long as she'd allow. What had been a cool, breezy night had now become humid again, and this time, it had nothing to do with the late-summer Georgia temperatures.

By the time he eased away from her lips, he almost expected a puff of steam to escape his shirt collar. "Eden…" He ran his fingertips over her satin jawline. "I want you so badly."

She trembled beneath his touch but remained quiet save for her quickened breaths.

He toured her body with a gentle, questing hand. First, he trailed his fingertips down the bare skin of her arm, then let his open palm caress the fullness of her thigh just below the hem of her dress. She writhed, a soft whimper escaping her lips.

She shifted a bit, tucking her legs beneath her. "Blaine…we're playing with fire here."

"You're telling me." The fire had been smoldering inside him since the moment she'd walked into his office and accepted his offer of work. There would be no putting this fire out, and truthfully, he wanted it to blaze until it consumed them both. He continued to circle and tease the exposed skin of her thigh. "Your thighs are magnificent. What do you do at the gym…squats?"

She blushed. "Yeah… I do a lot of side-to-side lunges, too."

"It's working for you."

She closed her eyes, sucking in her lower lip as her skin tingled beneath his touch. "You're too much, Blaine."

"I know I'm a lot." He chuckled. "But I also believe you'll be able to handle me just fine."

She leaned in and kissed him, and moments later, they were caught up in the throes of passion again. His tongue tangled with hers as he explored the sweet cavern of her mouth. By the time the kiss ended, he could feel his blood rushing toward his lower half.

"If memory serves, you have a sweet spot right… about…here." He slid his index finger up the side of her throat, swirling it over her skin just beneath the tip of her diamond-studded earlobe.

She gasped.

He leaned in, flicking his tongue over the sensitive spot. He repeated the gesture until her soft sighs rose on the cool night air.

She shifted, moving out of his reach for a moment. But before he had a chance to miss her, she slid into his lap, her full, lush hips resting atop his pelvis. By now he was so hard he could drive railroad spikes without a hammer, and he knew she could feel it.

He looked into her eyes in the moonlight.

She offered him a sultry smile. "You seem…excited."

He cleared his throat. "No hiding that. Especially not with you sitting on my lap like this." Running his hand over her silken waves, he growled, "Look what you're doing to me, Eden."

She winked. "I can do even better than that…but not

here." She gestured around with her hands, reminding him of where they were.

"You're right." He gave her hip a firm squeeze. "I'm pretty sure getting busy in the park is a quick way to get arrested."

She giggled, and the tinkling sound of her laughter warmed his heart. "Why don't we head over to my place, and we can…" The loud ringing of his phone, accompanied by its insistent buzzing, cut him off midsentence. Annoyed, he shifted and dragged the phone out of his back pocket, careful to keep Eden in her position on his lap. Looking at the screen, he frowned. *Geez. Nia's timing is absolute garbage.* His eldest sister rarely ever called him, and even when she did, it wasn't this late. Thinking he'd better take the call, he swiped the screen. "Hello?"

"Blaine, it's Nia. Stop what you're doing and come to Emory hospital right away."

He sat up straight, feeling the prickles of worry racing up his back. "What's going on? Has something happened?"

"It's Mom," Nia blurted, her tone grim. "She's been in an accident."

"What? How did it happen? And is she okay?"

"Blaine, I don't have time to give you a lot of detail right now. Just get down to the hospital as soon as you can, all right?"

He heard something in his sister's voice he'd never heard before. *Panic.* "I understand. I'll be there right away." Disconnecting the call, he looked at Eden and found her watching him, her expression etched with concern.

"I wasn't eavesdropping, but I can tell by your face that something's going on, something you need to attend to. Am I right?"

He nodded. "Yes. It's an emergency."

She slipped from his lap, then stood, straightening her dress.

He was on his feet moments later. "You've gotta know that nothing else short of an emergency could have pulled me away from you. You do know that, right?" She gave a small nod, her gaze soft and sympathetic. "I believe you, Blaine."

"It's my mom. She's been in some kind of an accident, and my sister is playing it close to the vest. I need to get over there and check on her." He grasped her hand, brought it up for his kiss. "Come on. I'll walk you back to your car."

After navigating the gauntlet of parking in the deck, he headed straight for the hospital information desk, hoping to find out more about his mother's condition.

Gage stood near the desk, his expression serious. "Hey, B. Nia sent me down here to meet you."

"Where's Mom?"

"She's in a room on the seventh floor. Get your visitor's pass and I'll take you up there."

He turned to the desk attendant, and after presenting his driver's license and posing for a rather drab-looking photo, he slapped on his adhesive visitor badge and followed his brother to the elevator.

On the ride up, Blaine asked, "Gage, what happened to Mom?"

He frowned. "You mean Nia didn't tell you?"

"You know how she is. She just ordered me to get my ass over here, without telling me anything except that Mom had been in an accident."

Gage rolled his eyes. "Same old Nia. Anyway, Mom was out running and took a pretty bad fall. Her left ankle is totally screwed up, and she's got quite a few scrapes and scratches."

He cringed. *Sounds like she had a rough day.* "How is she now?"

"She seems to be doing okay. They've patched her up and given her pain meds." The elevator dinged, and Gage stepped out, holding his hand out so the doors wouldn't shut before his brother exited. "I'm sure she'll be glad to see you."

He wanted to protest but managed to hold back.

They walked down a quiet concourse, where the only sounds were the footsteps of scrub-clad nurses and the occasional blip emanating from a machine until they approached an open door. Gage stepped back to let Blaine enter first.

Inside the small room, he found his entire immediate family. All his siblings were crowded around his mother's hospital bed, while a tired-looking Caleb sat in the blue recliner wedged between the bed and the wall. There were Teagan and Miles, the babies of the family, fraternal twins who both possessed their mother's sense of humor and her zest for life. Hovering beside them was Nia, the eldest, whose personality echoed her father's serious, regimented nature. And then there was Gage, who was only eleven months younger than Blaine. They were the closest in age and the only two of the kids who seemed to take their traits almost equally from both parents.

In the center of it all, Addison Woodson lay dozing in her bed. She was attached to a heart monitor, and the steady blips coming from the machine gave Blaine a measure of comfort. But the various bandages covering her arms, legs and the left side of her face, as well as the contraption stabilizing her ankle, were a worrisome sight. Not wanting to frighten her, he approached the bed quietly, easing in between the twins to get closer, and called out softly. "Mom?"

She opened her eyes slowly, and a smile spread over her face. "Blaine. Hi, baby."

Emotion welled in his chest. "Mom, are you all right?"

"I'm fine," she insisted in a sleep-heavy voice. "Should have turned down my music. Didn't see that cyclist coming until he was about to hit me." She yawned. "Dived out of his way—and right into a sticker bush."

He sighed. "Mom, you're a real pistol."

"You bet your ass. And don't you worry... I'll be back on the trail in no time." No sooner than the words left her mouth, she drifted back off to sleep.

Spotting an empty folding chair in the corner of the room, he took a seat. Now that he knew she was okay, he planned on staying put to hear what the doctors had to say.

His thoughts shifted briefly to Eden. His ardor for her would have to be set aside for the moment, but he planned on rectifying that as soon as possible.

Ten

Sunday evening, Eden chewed her lip as she knocked on the front door to Blaine's Ansley Park condo. The complex he lived in was less than ten minutes away from Piedmont Park; she'd been passing his place for ages without even knowing he lived there.

Ever since he'd buzzed her in at the gate, she'd been nervously fidgeting, wondering what tonight might hold. Would he really want to pick up where they'd left off the night before? Or would he still be distracted by whatever emergency had called him away in the middle of their rendezvous? She willed herself to stop over-thinking. *Guess I'll just play it by ear.*

She took a deep, soothing inhale, detecting the subtle but delectable aroma of garlic and herbs coming from his unit. Just as she released her breath, his door swung open.

"Hi, Eden." A welcoming smile stretched his full lips, revealing his pearly white teeth.

He looked comfortable but put together in a charcoal-gray button-down, dark slacks and black loafers with a silver chain detail across the toe box. The top three buttons of the shirt were left open, and the short sleeves revealed the muscled beauty of his biceps. His locs were piled on top of his head in a messy bun-slash-ponytail.

"Hey, you." She extended the silk pouch holding the bottle of merlot she'd brought. "A little gift to thank you for inviting me over."

"Thanks." He took the bag, then stepped aside and gestured her in.

She entered his domain, letting her gaze move around the interior. *Wow. This place is stunning.* The open floor plan gave her a wide-angle view of the polished oak floors and cabinetry, contrasted against the gray marble countertops and stainless appliances in the generously sized kitchen. He'd furnished the living room with a sleek but comfortable-looking camel-colored sofa, two matching chairs and a low-profile glass coffee table. "Nice place."

"Thanks. Bought it a few years ago." He walked around the tall granite-top bar that represented the only separation between the living room and kitchen, gesturing her to follow him. "It's close to the studio, spacious, and best of all, I don't have to cut the grass." He positioned himself by the stove, tending to something sizzling in a cast-iron skillet.

She chuckled as she eased onto one of the two uphol-stered wrought iron barstools. "I can see the appeal of that. I usually get one of the teenagers down the street to mow ours."

"Dinner should be ready in about fifteen minutes." He used his spatula to flip whatever was in the skillet.

"What are you making, anyway? It smells heavenly."

He used a mitt to grasp the pan's handle and gently shook it. "My vegan soul food specialty. Salisbury steak and mushroom gravy."

She pursed her lips, contemplating that. "Vegan steak? What's in that? And when did you become vegan?"

His deep rumbling chuckle preceded his answer. "The base for the steak is chickpeas and lentils. Don't worry, you'll love it. And I'm not vegan, but I try to eat three to four plant-based meals each week."

"I see." She looked down, suddenly self-conscious about her little lower-belly pooch. "So that's how you maintain that glorious physique, huh?" If eating fake steak made from legumes kept his body looking like it was carved from marble, she certainly wasn't going to knock it.

"I don't think I've ever heard my body called 'glo-rious' before. You flatter me, Eden." He tossed a wink over his shoulder.

She rolled her eyes for show. But deep inside, she fought off the urge to grab a handful of that magnifi-cent ass of his.

"But, nah. I work out to keep my body in shape. The way I eat is more about how I feel. I'm too old to be eating garbage, you know. Can't digest it. It's just not worth having an upset stomach."

"Relatable. I gave up fast food a few years back, and my insides are sincerely grateful." Giving up fast food, along with her regular strolls around the neighborhood, had helped her shave off a few pounds. Still, her curvy frame always seemed to hold on to a nice layer of padding, and she'd long since accepted the fact that she'd never be skinny. And that suited her just fine. "I'm looking forward to trying your creation."

"You're gonna love it. It's a big hit with Gage, and he loves meat to an almost frightening degree."

She nodded. As he worked at the stove, she couldn't help noticing the slight slump to his broad shoulders. "Hey, I'm not trying to get in your business, and you don't have to tell me anything if you don't want to. But what happened last night? Is everything okay?"

He turned off the burner and set down the spatula, facing her. "I don't mind telling you. My mother took a bad fall while out running yesterday evening."

She frowned. "Oh, no. Is she going to be all right?"

"She'll be fine. She's a real pistol, my mom. She's pushing sixty and you can't tell her anything." He shook his head, wearing a rueful smile, and quickly relayed how his mother had gotten hurt.

"Well, damn." Since she frequented the city's trails, she could easily imagine having such a run-in with an oblivious cyclist. "How's she holding up?"

"Other than being mad she can't run for a few weeks, she's in pretty good spirits. They kept her overnight because her pulse was erratic and the doc wanted to observe her, but they cut her loose this morning." He opened the fridge, pulled out two bottles of water and slid one to Eden. "Sent her home this morning with a cane, meds and orders to take it easy for a while." He cracked open the bottle, taking a big swig of water.

"How's the family handling things?" She opened her water and let its cold freshness quench her parched throat. Her other thirst, however, could only be satisfied by the man standing just beyond her reach.

"As well as can be expected. Nia's gone into 'bossy-britches' mode, but then again that's her default setting."

She snorted. "Bossy-britches?"

"If you ever meet my sister, trust me, you'll see what I mean." He took another sip from his water. "The twins are waiting on Mom, babying her the way she's always babied them. Gage, he's a little standoffish. I think it's hard for him to see Mom laid up like this. As for my Dad, he's giving her moral support."

"What about you, Blaine? How are you holding up?"

His eyes met hers. "It's not an ideal situation. I was pretty freaked out by Nia's cryptic call. But now that I know Mom will be fine, I feel better." He stifled a yawn. "I'm just a little tired and achy. I stayed at the hospital with Mom last night, and those damn hospital recliners will have your whole body in knots."

"I'm familiar." A memory passed over her mind like a storm cloud, of sitting at her aunt's bedside after the bus accident. Her mother had perished in the ambulance, but her aunt had held on for a few hours after the crash. Her final words still echoed in Eden's mind.

Take care of my Ainsley.

Shaking the memory off, she said softly, "Is it ready? I'm eager to test your skills in the kitchen." There was a double meaning there, and they both knew it.

He watched her, letting her remark hang between them for a moment before replying. "It's ready. I was just letting it cool off." He held her gaze for a long, smoldering moment. "We wouldn't want to get down before it's time, right?"

She sucked her lower lip between her teeth as a tingle of anticipation danced down her spine.

Seated at his beautifully set dining room table, she watched as he placed the finished plate in front of him. The pristine white bone china plate held the whipped mashed potatoes, running with mushroom gravy and topped with his vegan steaks. A pile of bright, crisp green beans, sautéed with shredded carrots and red onion, accompanied the main course. "Wow. This looks amazing."

He grinned as he took his seat across from her. "Wait until you taste it."

She dug in and soon found herself groaning with delight as the flavors collided on her tongue. "Blaine. You're a fantastic cook. This is really delicious."

His smile widened. "I'm glad you like it."

"I love it." She forked up more of the scrumptious offerings.

As they ate, they chatted about their day, the weather and the horrors of Atlanta traffic.

Before she knew it, she'd cleaned her plate. Setting her utensils down, she noted how she felt full, but not stuffed. "What a meal. I can't even imagine what you came up with for dessert."

"Oh, it's definitely the sweetest, the creamiest, the most delicate thing I could think of."

Her mouth watered at the prospect of whatever culinary delight he had in store. "Ooooh. What is it?"

Their gazes connected across the table.

"You."

Blaine felt the change in the atmosphere as soon as the word left his mouth. The air between them seemed to vibrate, saturated with the electric charge of their attraction.

Ever since she'd stepped over the threshold in that long, flowing fiery red dress, with slits on either side that parted to show off her luscious legs as she walked, he'd been keeping a tenuous hold over his hormones. She made him feel like a young man just discovering the birds and bees...and she was the only flower in the garden he wanted to buzz around.

Eden's eyes widened for a moment, then surprise melted into seduction as her glossy lips parted. She pushed her plate away, easing her chair back from the table. "Oh, really? And what makes you so sure I'll agree?"

"If you don't, I'll be devastated." He spoke softly as he stood and rounded the table. When he reached her chair, he knelt at her feet. He lifted one, observing the jeweled sandals she seemed to favor as he held her ankle in his hand. "All I ask is that you let me plead my case as to why you should."

Her tongue darted out, slid over her bottom lip. "And will I like the way you plead, Blaine?"

She was teasing him, and they both knew it. As hard as he was, he still savored every moment of this banter, this delicious back-and-forth. He caressed her ankle, then let his fingertips trail up to her calf. "You'll love it. I promise."

"Mmm." The low moan escaped her throat, spurring him onward.

He stroked her soft-skinned legs, grazing his open palms from her calves to the tempting fullness of her thighs. "You're so beautiful...so soft."

She let her head drop back.

He unfastened the jeweled sandals and set them aside. Sitting down, he took her bare feet into his lap and began massaging them with slow, methodical purpose. He worked each gold-painted toe in a small circle, then moved on to knead the instep of each foot.

She crooned in response. "Oooh. How did you know I needed a foot rub?"

"Psychic, I guess." He continued his work, feeling her muscles loosen beneath his touch. Her hips edged forward on her seat as she arched her back in response to his ministrations. Watching and feeling her reactions made him feel powerful...with each moment, he grew more confident that he'd be able to please her in all the ways she craved.

He stopped a moment before she would have slid off the chair, and her body made a slow return to its original positioning. She looked his way with passion-hooded eyes. "You make a very convincing argument," she whispered, reaching out to stroke his jawline.

As she leaned forward, the tops of her full breasts moved into his direct line of vision, and his dick pulsed with need.

He placed his hand atop hers. "I'm just getting started, baby."

She gave him a wicked smile. "Well, don't let me stop you."

He leaned forward, placing a series of soft kisses on the exposed swell of her bosom, enjoying the way she hummed with pleasure. "May I?" He grasped the thin straps of the dress, and she nodded. Letting the straps fall, he tugged the top of the dress down until the fabric bunched around her waist. His breath escaped in a whoosh as her full, naked breasts were revealed to his appreciative eyes. Unable to hold back, he took one rounded globe in each hand, giving them a gentle squeeze before devouring one taut, dark nipple.

Her small, sharp cries punctuated each suck, each lick, each pass of his thumb over her berried flesh. He kept his eyes open, thrilled by the sight of her, arched and trembling as he pleasured her.

He moved away for a moment, stood to kick off his loafers.

She was on her feet a moment later, tugging at the buttons of his shirt. A couple of them flew off, but he couldn't have cared less.

There in his dining room, with the moonlight streaming in through the window, they undressed each other. She undid the clasp of his pants as he tugged down her dress; undergarments followed, adding to the pile of fabric he kicked under the table. Once they were both as nude as the day they'd been born, she reached out, running her open palms over his abdomen.

His skin burned at this first tentative touch. She was gentle, tenderly caressing him, driving him mad with wanting. He pulled her into his arms, weaving his fingertips through her silken tresses as he lifted her face to his kiss.

Long, torrid moments passed as he savored the sweetness of her mouth. Yet there was another treat he wanted to taste, to devour. So he eased her back into her chair and knelt before her again. Hands guiding her into the proper positioning, he eased her hips forward and her thighs apart. He could see her glistening with wetness in the shadowy light, and he trailed his index finger over her hardened clit.

She gasped. "Blaine..."

"Don't worry, baby, I'll take care of you." He circled the taut bud, teasing it with his finger as he planned to do with his tongue. Moments later, he cupped the undersides of her thighs, raising and opening them further as his outstretched tongue delved between her slick folds.

She cried out, then dissolved into melodic moaning as he feasted on her. She was dripping with honey and tasted much sweeter than anything he could have concocted in his kitchen. There wasn't a finer dessert to be had anywhere in Atlanta, or the rest of the world, for that matter. While she writhed and sang her pleasure, he sucked, he teased, he enjoyed. Only when her orgasmic shout sliced the air did he stop.

He sat on the floor, watching her shiver and listening to her heavy breaths for a few moments before he stood. Grasping her hand, he asked softly, "Can you stand?"

"Mmm." Still trembling, she shook her head.

"I got you." He lifted her naked frame into his arms and carried her to his bedroom. Then, laying her atop the comforter, he sheathed himself with protection and eased between her parted thighs.

She grasped his hardness, her eyes locked with his as she guided him inside her warm, slick passage.

He groaned as he entered her fully. She was so hot and so gloriously tight. Her body gripped his shaft as he began to move, sliding in and out of her. Her fingernails dug into his back, but he ignored the sting as he worked his hips forward, then back, then forward again. Being inside her again after all this time felt so amazing, so right...he never wanted this to end.

"Oh, Blaine..." Her voice cracked as she called his name.

He couldn't recall ever hearing a sweeter sound.

And there, fourteen floors above the jewel of the South, he made love to her until exhaustion forced them to seek sleep.

Eleven

Monday morning found Eden standing in the studio at Against the Grain. Arms folded over her chest, she stood behind Trevor as he worked the soundboard. Next to Trevor sat the legendary hip-hop producer Jerome Dupois. Wearing a red-and-tan leather letterman jacket emblazoned with his famous label's logo, Jerome scribbled notes onto a notepad he'd brought in with him. Glancing his way, Eden wondered if and how the brotha could see more than a few inches in front of him, considering the dark sunglasses obscuring his eyes.

On the other side of the glass partition, Naiya sat atop the wooden stool inside the sound booth. Wearing the special noise-canceling headphones that allowed her to hear playback of the track unencumbered by outside interference, she shuffled through the pages of her lyric sheets.

Trevor, the engineer, was a laid-back dude with a close fade dressed in his standard uniform of white polo and khakis. Holding down the intercom button on the panel, he asked, "Naiya, you ready in there? I'm gonna feed the playback into your headphones, okay?"

She gave him a thumbs-up, straightening her posture on the stool.

Eden took a seat on the plush sofa behind the board, and the playback started just as she settled in. The mid-tempo track, featuring Dupois's signature funky bass line and rocking percussion, provided the perfect backdrop for the song. Eden's lyrics, inspired by the words in Naiya's journals, recalled the giddy excitement of the singer's first love.

She felt the smile tugging the corners of her lips as she heard Naiya's delivery. Her vocal talents were impressive, and she delivered a great first run-through of the song. As the track came to an end, Eden returned to the board and held down the intercom button on the soundboard.

"Wow, Naiya. You really can blow, girl!"

Naiya blushed. "Thanks, Eden."

She smiled. "I only have a few pointers for this next take. We'll run through the main melody once more before we move on to recording the harmonies." She checked her phone for the time. "We've still got about forty-five minutes before the backup singers get here, which should give us plenty of time."

"Okay, what do you need me to do?" Naiya lifted the left earphone, propping it haphazardly atop her head.

"Stretch that initial note just a little bit. When you get to the bridge, take it up a half an octave. And keep emoting—you're doing great putting your feelings into the music, okay?"

"I got it." Naiya returned the earphone to its proper position. "I'm ready."

Jerome raised his index finger and made a circling motion, signaling Trevor. The engineer restarted the playback, and Naiya leaned into the mic to belt out the song for a second time. Save for a random sneeze that caused one section to have to be rerecorded, she delivered a flawless second take.

Eden applauded as Naiya hung up her headset and exited the booth. "Amazing. Absolutely amazing. You've made light work for the backup singers."

Naiya stood in the doorway of the soundboard vestibule. "Thanks." She slipped her phone from the back pocket of her jeans. "You think I have time to run down for a quick coffee and a snack before the other girls get here?"

Eden nodded. "Sure. Besides, you've earned a break."

"Cool." Naiya called out to the producer, who was scrolling through his phone. "Yo, JD, you want anything?" Moments later, after promising the producer an herbal tea, she left.

Eden exited the studio soon after. Her mind wandered to Blaine, and the amazing encounter they'd had. She'd remained in his arms all night, and it was some of the best sleep she'd had recently. She smiled at the thought of the way he'd worked her body...and the way he'd greeted her the next morning with kisses and that beautiful smile. There was none of the awkwardness she'd been afraid of, but she hadn't been thrilled to hear him talk about how being with her brought back sweet memories. It made it seem as if he'd been reaching for the past, instead of working toward a future with her. Whatever the case, she knew she wanted to experience his lovemaking again, as soon as possible.

It took considerable effort, but she turned her thoughts back toward the work at hand.

I can't wait to tell Blaine about the amazing progress we're making on Naiya's album. Even seasoned music veterans often needed several takes to record a song; despite her young age and relative inexperience in a professional studio, Naiya consistently delivered her vocals in three takes or fewer. This was the third single they'd recorded so far, and if they could maintain this pace, they might actually be able to meet Blaine's rather unreasonable demand to finish the album before the month ended.

She walked down the hallway toward Blaine's office at the end. His door stood slightly ajar, and as she approached, she slowed. The sound of his voice filtered through the gap between the door and the frame.

She raised her hand to knock, but let it drop when she heard a familiar name.

Cambria. He's talking to her on the phone.

Resting her back against the wall, she felt the cool painted concrete against her bare shoulders. She shivered, wishing she'd brought a sweater to wear over her favorite pink T-strap maxi dress. Wondering what reason Blaine had to be talking to her former groupmate, she folded her arms and listened.

"I'm glad you called, Cambria," Blaine said, then paused, probably to listen to Cambria's reply. "Yes, actually, your timing is great. Guess who I'm working with?"

Eden frowned. *I've got a pretty good idea where this is going.* But would he really take it there? Or was she just projecting her worries onto him and his conversation?

"No. Nope. Listen, you're terrible at guessing so I'll just tell you." His tone held unveiled amusement. "It's Eden...yes, that Eden." He laughed. "No, no. All is forgiven. We're both mature adults, you know." He laughed again, this time more heartily. "I'm not going into details, Cambria. But trust me. We're definitely back on great terms. Probably even better than before." Her chest tightened, and a sense of dread rolled over her like a fog.

"No, no, it's true," he continued. "Listen, if you don't believe me, you can always slide through the 404 and see for yourself. When's the next time you're free to come down south?"

Eden sighed, her frown deepening. Turning away from the door, she went back toward the studio. She'd heard quite enough of Blaine's overblown characterization of their current partnership. From their chat the morning after they'd made love, she gathered their lovemaking was a means to relive the old days...to experience the heady sensations of their former relationship, for old time's sake. That's where he stood…and she told herself she could accept that. But could she?

Back then, he'd held the promise of a solo career over her like the proverbial carrot. But when the management decided Cambria was their golden girl instead, she'd been tossed aside. Eden had found it very karmic that Cambria had taken an offer from another label and gone on to stardom.

She walked into the studio long enough to grab her purse and strode right back out. As she headed outside to her car, her annoyance grew with each step. Not only was Blaine on the phone evangelizing about how great things were between them, but it seemed like he was using her and their so-called "great relationship" as some kind of weird bait to get Cambria to come to Atlanta. By the time she flung open her driver's-side door and climbed into her car, she could feel her body vibrating with hurt and anger.

Naiya, in her little blue two-door coupe, pulled into the spot next to Eden. Letting down her passenger-side window, she cast a confused glance her way. "You leaving already? I thought we were going back to work on the backing vocals?"

She blew out a breath, trying to calm herself. There was no reason to take her bad mood out on Naiya. "Sorry, but I need a little break. JD and Trevor are still in the studio… I'm sure they've got it covered."

"Okay." Naiya's expression showed her lingering questions, but thankfully, she refrained from asking any as she got out of her car. "I'll see you later."

Eden watched as Naiya went inside the building with

a cardboard carrier holding several drinks. She stuck the keys in the ignition but didn't start the car...she didn't even know where to go. Dropping back against the headrest, she let her mind wander back to those old days. Back when she, Ainsley and Cambria had been thick as thieves, a nearly inseparable trio. From the day they'd met at the beginning of their first year at Atlanta Tech, nothing had ever managed to come between them.

That was, until Blaine. He'd gotten them to record together the first time by capitalizing on their obvious closeness. Then, just as everything had seemed to be coming together for Swatz Girlz, just when they thought their careers were about to take off...he'd hit them with a ton of bricks.

And all these years later, he still couldn't seem to acknowledge the betrayal he'd dealt her, the way he'd shattered the heart of an idealistic, starry-eyed young woman. It wasn't just the end of her singing career; it was a death of her younger, more trusting self, an end to her naïveté.

A tear slid down her cheek, and she angrily swiped it away. *He's caused me enough pain. I'm not about to let him cause me any more.*

Blaine absently spun his chair from side to side, holding his phone to his ear as he listened to Cambria rambling on about her hectic schedule. He chuckled. "Okay, I get it. You can't get down here over the next couple of weeks, it's cool. Just hit me up when you get ready to come through."

"I will," Cambria insisted, "because I still don't believe you're on all these wonderful terms with Eden."

"Why not?"

She chuckled. "If you were a woman, you wouldn't even be asking me that question. You'd know the answer, man."

He rolled his eyes. "Whatever. Anyway, I'll let you get back to work. I'm gonna head down to the studio and look in on what's happening with Naiya B.'s album."

"Later, Blaine." Cambria disconnected the call.

He pocketed his phone, shaking his head. *Cambria Harding...the one that got away.* Professionally, at least. He'd harbored no romantic interest in her, but he'd known from the moment he'd met her that she possessed an amazing voice and incredible stage presence. Her star had risen quickly as a solo artist, and after her first album, she'd moved on to a larger label, one that could get her the kind of wide exposure she sought. He couldn't hold that against her. After all, her talent warranted the kind of massive backing she got from her internationally known label. She performed in huge arenas, drawing crowds of thousands of screaming fans wearing her custom-designed merchandise. As hard as he worked, he knew he simply didn't have those kinds of resources.

Standing up, he stretched his arms above his head before leaving his office. A few long strides carried him to the studio, and when he opened the door, he saw the work on Naiya's album continued. Naiya was on the couch, while JD and Trevor sat at the soundboard.

Inside the booth, two backup singers were recording vocals as the track playback echoed through the room.

However, he couldn't help noticing one rather conspicuous absence. "Where's Eden?"

Neither Jerome nor Trevor knew where she was. So he turned to Naiya. "Do you know where our songwriter is?"

She shrugged. "Not really. I ran into her in the parking lot, on my way back from the coffee shop. She said she needed a break."

His eyes widened. "I'll be back." He left the studio and jogged out to the parking lot. For some reason, the idea of her leaving in the middle of the day upset him. He hadn't gotten to spend very much time with her outside of the studio, and since they'd made love yesterday, she haunted his mind like a specter.

Outside, he stepped off the sidewalk and saw her sitting in her car, her eyes closed. Was she taking a nap? Part of him didn't want to disturb her, but he also wanted to know what had brought her out here in the first place, just in case he might be able to help. He tapped the glass, and her eyes popped open.

He saw the sheen of wetness in her eyes, and it tugged at his heart.

Her expression flat, she rolled the driver's-side window down.

"You okay? It's too hot outside for you to be sitting out here like this."

She frowned. "You picked a fine time to be concerned about me."

He felt his brow furrow. "What do you mean by that?"

She scoffed, shaking her head. "Why bother?"

"Eden, tell me what's wrong. If there's something I can do to fix it, I'll do it."

She gave him a sidelong glance. "Oh, really? Then explain to me why I heard you on the phone telling Cambria that we're besties now?"

He swallowed hard. "You were eavesdropping on my phone conversation?"

She pursed her lips. "No. Your office door was open and you're a loudmouth. I can't be blamed for you not knowing how to use your inside voice."

His hands clenched. "Whatever the case, you had no right to be listening in on my…"

"Whatever, Blaine. I couldn't care less who you talk to on the phone. The problem I have is what you're saying about me, about us."

"And what exactly did I say that you have such a problem with?"

"Why were you telling Cambria that all's well between us now? And from what I heard, it sounded like you were using our new 'liaison' as bait to lure Cambria back to Atlanta."

He thought back to his conversation, and it occurred to him that what he'd said might have sounded flippant and dismissive of her feelings. "Eden, I don't know what to say that's going to satisfy you. But I really thought we were making great progress."

She released a bitter chuckle. "Why? Because we made love?"

He wondered if his expression conveyed his confusion. "Wow. Really, Eden?"

She sighed. "Yes, really, Blaine. You really haven't been listening to me all this time, have you?"

"I've heard everything you've said."

"But you haven't listened. Because if you had, you'd know where I'm coming from." She shook her head.

He shifted his weight from foot to foot, crammed his hands into his pockets. This again? Hadn't he told her more than once that his hands had been tied? That he'd had to make a hard decision for the sake of his business? "You can't still be talking about being cut. It's been years, Eden."

She fixed him with a hard stare. "Blaine, you're treading on thin ice. Do you really wanna keep going down this road?"

He sighed. "No, I don't. At least not now."

She pursed her lips. "I didn't think so."

"Don't get me wrong, Eden. I'm not avoiding this argument you seem so determined to have with me. All I'm doing is postponing it because now isn't the right time."

"Oh, really? So tell me, Blaine. When exactly *is* the right time?"

He shrugged. "I can't give you an exact date. All I'm saying is, can we please, please finish Naiya's album before you proceed with chewing my head off?"

She scowled.

"I know you don't think I deserve the courtesy, and maybe you're right." Part of him still couldn't grasp what had her so irrationally angry, but after hearing the same thing from her so many times, he was beginning to wonder if there might be things he hadn't considered. Still, he didn't want to see Naiya's project flushed down the tubes because of whatever personal drama existed between him and Eden. "But Naiya does. She's been working so hard, grinding day and night so this album can finally come to fruition. Don't do it for me. Do it for her, okay?"

Eden's expression softened, and she appeared thoughtful for a moment. Finally, she spoke. "Fair enough. After all, it was work that brought me here, and if I want to keep my reputation as a songwriter intact, I have to remain professional, no matter what."

"Thank you." He pulled the handle to open her car door, then bowed.

She stepped out, rolling her eyes. "Okay, Mr. Dramatics. Let's get back inside and check on Naiya's progress. It'll be lunchtime soon, and we need to see if Jerome is hungry. He's been with us all morning."

He chuckled. "Somebody's gonna have to go down to Midtown for him. You know he's vegan, right?"

"I didn't know that." She walked ahead of him toward the door, and he found it hard not to stare at her ass, the curve of which he could see through the flowy fabric of her dress.

"Yep. I'm full of fun facts. You'll learn a lot of stuff if you just hang around me a while longer." He reached out and opened the door, holding it so she could enter.

"We'll see, Blaine. We'll see."

Twelve

Eden spent the rest of the day keeping her distance from Blaine and focusing on her work. Jerome left a little after lunch to go about the rest of his day, while Trevor worked his editing magic on the backing vocals recorded by the two hired singers. Eden remained on the sofa behind the soundboard, observing Naiya's work and giving pointers whenever necessary. Blaine came into the room a few times to converse with Trevor, but each time he looked her way, Eden made a point of turning her gaze elsewhere.

Around five thirty, with one finished track and the rough cuts of two more committed to digital memory, Trevor stifled a yawn. "Okay, folks. Let's pack it in."

"You don't have to tell me twice." Naiya took off her headset and placed it in its cradle. "I'm so hungry you may have to edit my stomach rumbling out of the music."

Eden chuckled. "Same. Come on out of there. You've done fantastic work today."

After the equipment had been shut down and secured, and the lights turned off, Naiya and Trevor left the building. Eden stopped by the restroom and was on her way out the door when she caught a whiff of expensive cologne. She stopped mid-step. Feeling a familiar presence entering her space, she slowly turned—and came face-to-face with Blaine. She let herself drink in the sight of him, for the first time today. He wore a crisp white button-down, top button undone, beneath a studded leather jacket. Fitted black jeans sat low on his hips, and the black motorcycle boots on his feet were tipped with silver toe caps. His shades were perched atop his head, and his amber eyes burned into hers.

"What is it?" She was perturbed at being waylaid from going home to curl up with a mug of tea and a good book, and she didn't bother to hide that from her tone.

"Remember what I said earlier? About putting off arguing until later?"

She narrowed her eyes. "Yeah, I remember."

"Well, it's later." He stood there watching her expectantly.

"Blaine, not now. I'm too tired to fight. I just want to go home."

He reached out and grasped her hand. "You don't

have to fight. I just want you to give me a chance to try to smooth things over between us."

She pursed her lips. "And just how do you plan on doing that?"

He smiled as he guided her down the darkened hallway toward his office. "You'll see."

She sighed but followed him anyway. Something about him drove her wild, made her cast aside her good sense in favor of spending time with him. He'd worked his way into her heart again, despite all the barriers and obstacles she'd erected to keep him out. And as much as she wanted to fight it, she knew it was a losing battle.

Blaine Woodson had a hold on her, one she couldn't seem to shake.

He turned the knob with his free hand, pushing open the door to his office and gently tugging her inside. He'd cleared his desk, save for his thin keyboard and flatscreen computer monitor. Patting the edge of the desk, he said, "Have a seat."

She did as he asked, perching her hips on the desk surface. "Is there anybody else in the building?"

He shook his head, then leaned in and kissed her, a soft, fleeting brush of his lips against hers. "There's no one here except you and me. That means we can settle this right now, without being disturbed."

"Blaine, whatever you're going to say, make it quick. I'm really worn out."

He released her hand then, sitting down in the guest chair. "Who said I planned on saying anything?"

Her eyes widened as he scooted the chair forward, his shoulders coming in line with her hips.

His fingertips grazed the bare skin of her ankles, then crept slowly upward as he moved up the fabric of her dress. "My mouth will be too busy for me to talk."

"Blaine." His name escaped her lips on a breathy sigh as his palm blazed a hot trail over her thigh. Her legs widened of their own accord in response to his touch.

"Yes?" he murmured into her thigh as he kissed it.

"Oh…" A tremor worked its way down her spine.

"Do you want me to stop, baby?" He swirled his tongue over her knee.

Her heart thundered in her ears, and the rising passion made her whimper, "No, don't stop…"

As he bunched the fabric of her dress around her waist, he eased aside her silky panties. Questing fingers stroked her, teased the bud of her womanhood until she flowed sweet and wet. Moving her hips in tandem with his ministrations, she felt herself slipping off the edge of the desk.

He steadied her with his free hand, and moments later, she felt his kiss between her thighs. She shuddered as he followed with a series of slow, deliberate licks and sweet, gentle sucks. He tossed one thigh over his shoulder, his tongue delving deeper. Her hips bucked, her back arched, and as the sensations grew to a crescendo, she screamed his name while the spreading warmth engulfed her entire being.

She returned to awareness, finding herself laid out across his desktop, her dress in disarray. When she looked down, she saw him sitting back in the chair, looking rather satisfied with himself. Sitting up, she straightened the garment and met his eyes. "Though they lack substance, your arguments are very convincing."

He grinned. "Thank you."

She shook her head, smiling in spite of herself. "Damn it, Blaine. Do you have a serious bone in your body?"

"Of course, I do." He gave her a wicked look and an exaggerated wink.

She licked her lips. The remnants of his masterful oral "argument" were still reverberating through her body, and she couldn't deny that she wanted more.

"I'll take that as a yes." He stood then, reaching for the zipper of his jeans.

She felt her breath catch in her throat. "You're not serious. We can't really…"

"What? Fuck in my office?" He tilted his head to the side. "Well, since I own this building, and everything in it, I'd say we can do whatever we damn well please."

A shiver tripped down her spine, and she bit her lip. "Oh, my."

By now he'd undone the jeans and pushed them down. His boxers quickly followed, and he left the fabric pooled around his hips. Moving forward, he grasped her hips, tugging her toward the edge of the desk.

She gasped when his hardness bumped against her inner thigh.

He worked the dress up around her waist again. Licking his lips, he leaned forward, his breath warm on her face. "Tell me again what we can't do in here?"

Her arousal level increased tenfold just from his tone

of voice. She knew she couldn't form a coherent sentence, so she simply purred into his ear.

He pecked her on the lips, then hurriedly fished a condom out of his back pocket. The moment he'd covered himself, he slipped his hands beneath her ass, cupping it as he raised her hips. Then he slid inside her in one long, delicious stroke.

She groaned, her back arching in response to him filling her so erotically. Her hands wrapped around his strong shoulders, she held on as he rocked his hips, each thrust sending her closer and closer to ecstasy.

"Eden...baby." He ground out the words in time with his thrusts. "So tight."

The shaking began then, beginning in her thighs and spreading through her whole body, as an orgasm sprouted and bloomed. Soon her impassioned cries and his rough grunts echoed through the empty building.

In the aftermath, he righted their clothing and pulled her into his lap, holding her close while she tried to slow her breathing.

"You're amazing," she admitted with a contented sigh.

"Does that mean you're not mad at me anymore?"

"It means what I said. I do need to get home, though." She knew what he was trying to do, and now that she had her wits about her, she wasn't about to play this game with him. Yes, Blaine was a magnificent lover. But that prowess wasn't a get-out-of-jail-free card he could use to erase his mistakes. *Maybe that's how he is with other women, but he's not going to do that to me.*

She knew she wasn't perfect. Hell, nobody was.

Growing up without a father in her life had made her somewhat cynical. She held on to things like the proverbial dog with the bone, and she made people work hard to earn her trust. Still, how could she be blamed for protecting her heart? If she didn't do it, who else would?

She stood, and finding her legs a bit wobbly, she waited for her knees to quit knocking together. Once she felt she had steady footing, she started walking. "Bye, Blaine. I'll see you tomorrow."

His exasperated groan followed her, but she didn't look back.

When Blaine walked into his condo Thursday night, Gage was already seated on the sofa in the living room. Their typical game-time snacks were artfully arranged on the coffee table, and Blaine could tell his brother hadn't seen fit to wait for his arrival before digging in.

"You're late," Gage called around a mouthful of popcorn.

"Good evening to you, too, bro."

Washing down the popcorn with a swig of cola, Gage chuckled.

"I never should have given you a key to my place." He shut the door behind him and hung his keys on the hook near the door. "Flattening out my couch cushions...eating my snacks..."

"You know you love me."

Snorting, Blaine joined his brother on the couch. "Why are you such a pain in the ass, Gage?"

"When we were kids, we went to the state fair one

year, and you tried to trade me in for cotton candy. Do you remember that?"

He frowned. "Not really." *Though I do love cotton candy, even to this day.*

"Neither do I, but ever since Mom told me the story, I've been looking for subtle ways to pay you back for it." He winked.

Blaine groaned. *Leave it to Gage to hold something like that against me.* "What did I miss?"

"The whole pregame show and kickoff, but not much else." He scooped up more popcorn from the ceramic bowl. "But I have to ask you a question."

"What?"

"Why haven't you been to the house to visit Mom? Ever since she got out of the hospital, she's been asking about you."

"I stayed at the hospital all night with her Saturday. Doesn't that count for something?"

Gage munched for a moment before speaking again. "Of course, it does. But she still wants to see you."

"I know Nia, the twins and Dad have probably been smothering her with attention." He turned his gaze toward the television, not wanting to meet his brother's accusing stare. "She doesn't really need me there."

"Oh, so now you get to decide what Mom needs?" Gage shook his head. "Why are you being so stubborn?"

Blaine twisted his mouth into a frown. "You'll have to excuse me for not wanting to be around the rest of the family. They're all judging me any time we get together, and I just don't want any part of it."

"Who says anybody is judging you?"

He scowled. "Oh, please. Nia told me as much herself, and I can tell the twins are judging me by the standoffish way they act. Trust me, I'm our parents' biggest disappointment."

Gage shook his head. "Blaine, you are way too dramatic. Anyway, I'm just passing a message along. If you don't go see Mom in the next three days, she said she's going to pluck you like a chicken."

He cast his brother a sidelong glance.

Gage shrugged. "Don't look at me like that. That was a direct quote."

He almost wanted to laugh, but he knew their mother was quite serious. Addison Woodson loved her children fiercely, but she never made idle threats. "I got it. I'll go visit her soon, I promise."

"Meanwhile, we need to talk about the real reason you're so distracted."

"What's that?" He braced for one of his brother's leaps to a conclusion.

"It's Eden, isn't it?"

He shifted uncomfortably in his seat. "Eden? What does she have to do with anything?"

Gage snickered. "Oh, please! I know you're involved with her."

"You don't know as much as you think you do, Gage."

"Whatever. I know that when I called you yesterday, you were at lunch with her."

"So? That doesn't mean..."

"And the day before that? Trevor told me you were locked in your office with her for at least two hours, and that when he left Monday, the two of you were still at the studio…alone."

Blaine rolled his eyes. "You pressing my employee for information now, Dick Tracy?"

"No, I'm not. But since Trevor and I play poker together on Tuesday nights, we talk." Gage fixed him with a penetrating stare. "It doesn't matter where I'm getting my information, we both know it's true. It's so obvious you're trying to pick up where y'all left off back in the day."

"If you're trying to make a point, just get to it already."

"Listen, I like Eden. We all do—she's a great person." Gage poked him in the shoulder with his index finger. "Don't screw her over this time, Blaine. Don't break her heart."

"You don't honesty think I'd set out to hurt her, do you?" He ran a hand through his locs. "Things just didn't work out, that's all."

Gage sighed. "I'm going to get some more soda." Standing with his empty glass in hand, he said, "You've got a lot of things going for you, bro. Self-awareness ain't one of 'em."

Blaine watched his brother walk away, shaking his head. *What is he going on about now? Sure, I made some mistakes the first time around with Eden, but who hasn't? Plus, I'm older and wiser now.* Gage was the middle child in every way possible: always analyzing his siblings' behavior, trying to outsmart them or trick them into holding hands and singing "Kumbaya." *As much as I love him, he is way too extra sometimes.*

Nevertheless, he thought about his brother's declaration that he lacked self-awareness. What did he mean by that, exactly? He considered himself very thoughtful in general, but especially when it came to his personal relationships and his business dealings. *Could a man without self-awareness have achieved this level of success in the music industry?* Especially one who'd eschewed his family's fortune and power to make his own way?

As for Eden, she was a grown woman, and capable of making her own decisions. *What's happening between Eden and me is none of Gage's damn business. So what if I don't know exactly where we're headed just yet? We'll figure it out.*

Thirteen

Friday morning, Eden sat next to Trevor at the sound-board, watching proudly as Naiya recorded her fifth single for the album. Hearing the way Naiya delivered her lyrics delighted her; every songwriter dreamed of working with someone with talent of this caliber.

Swaying along with the lilting music of the ballad, Eden couldn't help smiling. *This album is going to be a huge hit. I can feel it.* Though her relationship with Blaine still had its ups and downs, she didn't regret taking this job. In addition to being able to cover the cost of her roof in full, she knew working with Naiya would end up being very positive for her career. Then there was the glimmer of hope that she and Blaine could re-kindle their romance. There was something especially sweet about the second time around… Shalamar had written a whole song about it. But she needed to know he'd changed, that he understood how to really care for her heart.

As playback ended on the first run-through, Trevor turned on the intercom to communicate with Naiya in the booth. "Awesome take. Let's run it back a couple more times so you can record your harmonies. You want the high road or the low road first?"

"I'll do the soprano, then the tenor." Naiya adjusted her headphones, then gave the thumbs-up.

Just as Trevor restarted playback on the track, the studio door swung open. Blaine strode in, and Eden could feel her body aligning with the frequency of his presence in the space. This was her first time seeing him today, and she swallowed the warmth of arousal rising in her chest. He wore a pair of tight black jeans adorned with thin silver chains draped through the belt loops like a metallic bunting. His black shirt was printed with white music notes, and the buttons were open to reveal the yellow tank beneath. Black motorcycle boots on his feet and the ever-present lion's head necklace completed today's look.

As he moved into the soundboard suite, the scent of his cologne awakened her senses. Notes of wood, citrus and musk curled up her nostrils with each inhale, effectively undoing her concentration. She was so distracted by his handsomeness and his heady aroma; it took her several moments to realize he hadn't entered alone.

Blaine's companion was a stout, pale man in a black suit. The man had blue eyes and dark blond hair combed over in an attempt to conceal a receding hairline.

Eden stood from her chair as Blaine came near, with the stranger close on his heels.

"Morning, Eden. I want you to meet Marvin Samuels. He's the label liaison from Hamilton House."

He stuck out his hand. "I'm pleased to meet the songwriter Blaine's been going on about. How are you?"

She felt her cheeks warm when he mentioned Blaine's praise. "It's lovely to meet you as well, Mr. Samuels."

"Call me Marvin." He gave her a friendly wink.

With the introductions made, she watched as Blaine and Marvin took seats on the sofa. Returning to the soundboard, she asked, "So, what brings you to Atlanta, Marvin?"

"I had a few meetings in town, and I wanted to swing by and see our newest star in action." He gestured toward Naiya, who sat inside the booth, silently mouthing the words as she read over her lyric sheet.

"I see." She returned her attention to her own copies of the lyric sheets. In the back of her mind, she wondered what Marvin would think of Naiya. He seemed to be in a position of reasonable power at the label, and she had to assume his opinion would have some influence. Still, if he had any real experience in the industry, she figured he'd have to be pretty damn jaded to be unimpressed by Naiya's raw, natural talent.

She also noticed the way Blaine seemed to be reacting to Marvin's presence. His usual relaxed posture and easy smile had been replaced by a serious, businesslike expression and ramrod-straight posture. *Considering how deep and fluffy the couch is, it's got to be taxing for him to be sitting up that straight.* She smiled at the thought of the core strength he was building...strength she hoped to put to good use later.

The four people in the soundboard suite watched silently as Naiya worked through the song. This particular track had a higher level of complexity than the ones she'd previously recorded, requiring her to record several takes of each verse. While the music played, Eden made notes on the elements of Naiya's delivery that she picked up on.

Blaine seemed to be enjoying what he heard. Nodding his head along to the music, he remarked, "This ballad is fantastic. She's really bringing out all the feels on this track."

Eden had to agree. "She amazes me every time she steps in the booth."

As the session drew to an end about ninety minutes later, Naiya left the booth and came over to the soundboard suite. She walked over to the sofa and stuck out her hand. "Marvin. It's great to see you again."

"Likewise." He gave her a broad smile.

"Me and Trevor are going to grab lunch at the deli. Does anyone want anything?" Naiya took her purse from the hook by the door and slid the strap onto her shoulder.

They all shook their heads.

After Naiya and Trevor left, Eden went back to her notes. Behind her, she could hear Blaine and Marvin chatting. Listening to the way he talked about Naiya, the album and her lyrics made her feel wonderful.

"What did I tell you, Marvin? Isn't Naiya amazing?"

"That she is. Very impressive."

"I'm really excited about her project in general," Blaine announced. His eyes were alight, his hands gesturing as he spoke. "She's on the brink of something major—we could be looking at the beginnings of a stratospheric career. And I'm not just talking about the R & B market, either. She could go so much further than that, especially with a talented songwriter like Eden working with her."

"Hmm." Marvin nodded but said nothing.

Eden wasn't sure what to make of his reaction, but something about it stood out to her. She couldn't understand why Blaine's passion didn't seem to be rubbing off on the label exec. *Is it just me, or does Marvin seem a lot less excited about all this than Blaine does?*

"I really feel like Naiya could go mainstream if we just…"

Marvin cleared his throat loudly, effectively cutting him off in mid-sentence. "I wouldn't worry about all that right now, Blaine. You're broadcasting too far into the future. For now, just focus on helping Naiya do her best work and getting this album finished as quickly as possible, without sacrificing quality."

Even as he maintained a congenial smile, Blaine's shoulders slumped, and the sparkle faded from his eyes. "Sure thing, Marvin. Don't worry. I've got it covered."

The exec stood then. "I need to get going. I've got a few more meetings and then a late flight back to New York."

Blaine got to his feet as well, shaking hands with Marvin. "Thanks for coming by."

"No problem. I look forward to hearing the finished

product soon." Marvin turned and tipped an imaginary hat in her direction. "Lovely meeting you, Eden."

"Same here. Safe travels." She offered a small smile.

Not long after that, Marvin left. Alone in the soundboard suite with Blaine, she watched him. He stood in the middle of the room, staring off into space.

"Are you okay, Blaine?"

"Huh?" He glanced her way, his expression absentminded.

"I asked if you were okay." She watched him, awaiting his response.

He remained silent for a few moments, and even though he looked in her general direction, he almost seemed to be looking through her instead of at her. Finally, he shrugged. "I'm fine." Without any further explanation, he turned and left the suite.

Standing alone in the empty room, Eden felt her doubts resurface. She'd just watched as Blaine went from total rapture over their joint project to utter indifference. It was as if Marvin's lack of enthusiasm had effectively killed Blaine's.

Pulling the front door shut behind him, Blaine stepped into the grand foyer of his parents' Buckhead home. The palatial home of his youth, with its marble floors, Yoruba and Xhosa art pieces, and polished wood looked as immaculate as Lourdes, the housekeeper, always kept it. He stopped for a moment, listening for sounds that might indicate the presence of his father or siblings. He didn't hear any chatter or footsteps, so he assumed his family members were out and about, doing whatever they did on Saturday mornings. Leaving his shoes on the rack, he headed up the wide staircase to the second floor.

Turning left at the top of the staircase, he headed toward the open door of his mother's study. The soft sounds of jazz wafting from within gave away her probable presence there, and when he rapped softly on the door and peeked into the room, he confirmed his guess.

There she is.

Inside the small room, decorated in shades of melon, peach and pink, Addison Woodson reclined on her favorite embroidered chaise. She wore her favorite pink satin robe and a matching marabou slipper on her uninjured foot. Most of her body from chest down was adorned in one of her old, but clean, colorful afghans; her short gray curls were similarly wrapped in a blue silk scarf. A fragrant mug of jasmine tea on the table and a magazine in hand, she looked up at his entrance. "Blaine. I assume you got my message from Gage?"

He nodded. "Yes, Mama. And I had no desire to be plucked like a chicken."

She smiled. "Then you made the right decision in coming to visit me." She gestured to the armchair to the left of her. "Come here, honey, and sit with your mother for a little while."

He did as she asked, taking a seat in the plush chair. The soft cushion immediately sank beneath his weight, enveloping him. "How are you feeling, Mama? You're looking much better."

"Thank you, son." She yawned. "Now, once I get this ugly boot thing off my foot, I can go back to wearing the fashionable footwear I'm used to." She gestured down at her feet. "This one-shoe look is not hot."

"How long will you have to wear it?"

"Another month or so, depending on how well it heals." She sighed. "I miss going to the gym, running. Not to mention being able to dress up and put on a pair of nice pumps and go dancing with your father."

He noticed that a few of the bandages on her face were gone, and the remaining cuts and bruises were on their way to healing up. "I know it's hard, Mama. But try to be patient."

She set her magazine aside. "I *am* being patient. But a girl's got things to do."

"Like what? What's so pressing that Dad or one of us can't take care of it for you?" Blaine gave his mother a pointed look. "Now isn't the time to be overtaxing yourself."

"Fair enough, Blaine. I promise to rest…if you promise to answer one question for me."

One thing I know about Mama—she's unpredictable. He leaned back in the chair, bracing for whatever she might throw his way. "Sure. What do you want to ask me?"

"When were you going to tell me that Eden is back in the picture and that y'all are seeing each other again?"

His mouth fell open, and he blinked several times. "What? Who told you that?"

She pursed her lips. "I'm not about to reveal my sources. Anyway, who told me is beside the point. Why didn't you let me know she was back in your life again?"

He sighed. "Mama. It's not like that. She's a songwriter, and I asked her to work with me on a debut album for a new artist. That's it."

She folded her arms over her chest and gave him that knowing look only Black mothers gave their children. "Boy, do you think I just fell off the turnip truck? I know good and well that if she's been in your space, you've been in her face."

He closed his eyes, shaking his head. *She knows me so well she can rhyme about me like Dr. Seuss.* "Yikes, Mama. You gotta step on my throat like that?"

"Right now, I'm only stepping on your throat metaphorically, on account of this bad foot." She pointed at her boot. "But if you don't come clean, so help me, I'm gonna give you a swift kick with my good foot."

He blew out a breath. "I guess I'm busted."

"Very much so."

"Okay, Mama." He knew better than to keep denying her the information she sought. "I really did ask her to work with me on the album, and she's done a fantastic job with the lyrics. She's really captured Naiya B.'s essence as a singer and infused it into the music. It's amazing to see."

Addison rolled her eyes dramatically. "Yeah, yeah. I know Eden can run circles around a lot of these folks out here writing songs. That's not what I asked you about though, is it?"

Seeing that his mother planned on giving him no quarter, he said, "Fine, Mama. Yes, I'll admit it. The chemistry we had between us is still very much alive."

"Mmm-hmm."

"Come on, Mama. How much detail do you expect

me to go into here? This is getting embarrassing." If he said much more, he feared she might wash his mouth out with soap. No way would he be filling his mother in on the impure thoughts—and actions to match—that he'd had pertaining to Eden.

Her expression changed for a moment, into sort of a half frown. "You know what… I'm fine with that. Let's just say you're in love with her and leave it at that. Spare me the gory details."

He frowned. "Who said anything about being in love with her? All I said is we had chemistry."

She snorted a laugh. "Boy, you are hilarious. You can tell me you don't love her till you're blue in the face. Put it on a billboard. Have it written in the sky if you want. But it ain't gonna change reality."

Blaine dropped his face into his hands. He couldn't think of anything scarier than one of his mother's "declarations." She'd made plenty of them in his day, and he couldn't recall even once when she'd been wrong. Family lore had it that all the women on his mother's side were soothsayers. His great-grandmother, his grandmother and now his mother. Nia and Teagan seemed similarly gifted—if one could call it a gift—and he assumed that should he father a daughter, she'd continue the family tradition.

"Don't get quiet on me now, son."

"What can I say? We all know about your predictions, Mama."

"It's very mature of you not to fight it." She took a long sip from her mug of tea. "Very mature."

He sighed, rubbing a hand over his temple. Yes, he

was attracted to Eden. And yes, making love with her felt like a taste of heaven. But…love? What he'd felt for her all those years ago had certainly been love. He'd assumed the passage of time had effectively ended his feelings. Perhaps he'd been wrong. He couldn't imagine that being a good thing.

Emotions only served as distractions, or weaknesses to be taken advantage of. If he let his heart get involved, he knew for certain his feelings would be used against him.

And he simply couldn't let that happen.

Not now, not ever.

Fourteen

"Aunt Eden, did you hear me?"

"Huh?" Eden snapped back to reality at the sound of Cooper's voice insistently calling her name. "Sorry, honey, I wasn't paying attention. What did you say?"

He shook his head. "Auntie, do you need some coffee? You look kinda sleepy."

Stifling a yawn, she nodded. "Yes, sweetie. I could use some coffee." She had a serious case of the Mondays. She'd spent a good portion of the night tossing and turning instead of sleeping. And the few times she had drifted off, her dreams were filled with visions of Blaine, doing all kinds of naughty things to her. Now, even though she wasn't going into the studio until later, she was sitting in the lobby of her nephew's physical therapist, waiting for his name to be called. Ainsley couldn't get the day off, so despite her drowsiness, she'd driven him here. After his appointment, she'd deliver him to school, as any aunt worth her salt would.

"You know they have coffee over there." Cooper raised his small hand and pointed to an out-of-the-way alcove across the lobby.

Her eyes widened as she climbed to her feet. She'd been so focused on getting him here early, she hadn't even noticed the coffee station. "Bless you, Cooper." A few minutes later, she returned with a steaming cup of Colombian roast, doctored with her preferred amount of cream and sugar. Sliding back into her seat, she took the first long sip and groaned in delight. "Listen, I'm taking you for ice cream this weekend."

A broad grin spread across his face, and he started doing the Milly Rock right there in his seat. "Thanks, Auntie."

She winked, going back for another sip of coffee. The warm liquid trickled down her throat like velvet. She felt energized as the coffee slowly began to take effect. *Sweet, sweet caffeine.*

After another few minutes of her guzzling coffee and Cooper playing some kind of puzzle game on his phone, the nurse called his name. Grabbing her purse, Eden stood and extended her hand to Cooper.

"Ah, come on, Auntie. I'm too big for that now." He glanced around the lobby as if he were looking for someone.

"What, are you afraid one of your little friends is gonna just appear here and see you holding my hand?" She chuckled. "You're still not one hundred percent stable on your feet yet, Champ. Once you're steady, I'll let go, okay?"

He gave her a sheepish look. "Okay." He took her offered hand, and she helped him to his feet. His first few steps were a bit wobbly, as had been the case ever since his injury. But after ten or so, he seemed all right on his own, so she released his hand.

The nurse led them down the hallway to the gymnasium, where Dr. Lexi Madison, his therapist, waited. A petite black woman with an Afro, she wore her signature royal-blue scrubs embroidered with her name and the alphabet soup of all her various degrees.

"Morning, Cooper. How are you?" She walked over and extended her fist.

Cooper smiled and bumped fists with her. "I'm fine, Dr. M."

"Ready to get started on your exercises?"

He nodded. "Yeah. I've been practicing at home with Mom and Aunt Eden, too."

"Awesome." Lexi caught his arm and began leading him toward the obstacle course she'd set up for him.

Eden took her seat in one of the plush chairs bordering the space, where family members waited for the patients to complete their appointments. Phone in hand, she was scrolling through social media when she got a text from Blaine.

GM. Where are you?

She dashed off a quick reply. I'm at the PT with my nephew, remember?

I forgot. My bad. What time are you coming to the studio?

She rolled her eyes. *I told him all this Friday, but I guess he wasn't paying attention. He's awfully good at pretending to listen.* Around 11, after I take him to school.

I really want to see you.

She sighed. What did he mean by that? *I'm not about to ask him.* You will. In a few hours.

He responded with a "heart eyes" emoji, and she sucked her lip. *This man is gonna be the death of me.* Things between them had become so much like they'd been back in the day, and she found it both exhilarating and terrifying. Yes, she loved the way he made her body feel—the stolen kisses, the shared looks, the lovemaking. But her memory of what they'd shared back then would always be tainted by the reality of his betrayal, a reality he had yet to fully acknowledge.

Another text came in. Hey, what are you wearing? ;)

Wait and see, crazy. She tucked her phone away, determined not to answer any more of his cheeky texts. Instead, she focused on watching her nephew work through the tasks Dr. Madison had set out for him. He climbed up and down stairs, wove his way between cones and hula hoops, and rode the stationary bike. He'd healed well from the surgery and made it just in time for the last day of baseball tryouts. Now that he'd made the team, he worked even harder at his therapy exercises. It made her happy to see him so excited about playing baseball, and the way that excitement seemed to fuel his progress. *Pretty soon, he should be ready for prime time.*

At the end of the hour, Dr. Madison walked Cooper over to the chair where Eden sat. "He did very well today, Ms. Voss. I'm really pleased with his progress."

"Great." She brushed a fallen lock of hair away from her eyes. "Do you think he'll be ready to start training with the team in November?"

She nodded. "I don't see any reason he couldn't. As long as he continues to do his exercises and is careful not to reinjure that lower leg, he should be just fine."

"Yes!" That news had Cooper dancing again.

Eden laughed at her nephew's exuberance. "Thanks, Dr. M."

"No problem." She fist-bumped Cooper again. "See you next week, buddy."

After they left the office and she'd delivered her nephew safely to school, she headed back toward the studio. The benefits of two cups of coffee were flowing through her veins, and she finally felt awake. Still, she didn't know what to expect when she walked into the studio. She'd seen her share of famous folks coming and going, so she tried to make sure she looked presentable at all times. At least that's what she told herself, because she didn't want to accept that she might be spending so much extra time on her appearance because of Blaine.

She swung by the restroom just inside Against the Grain's building. There, she adjusted her navy slacks and the dolman sleeves of her white blouse, then checked her reflection in the mirror. Smoothing her hair behind her ears and adjusting her headband, she walked out of the bathroom...

And nearly crashed into Cambria.

Blaine trailed behind Cambria by a few steps as they left his office. He saw Eden headed in their direction, though she appeared to be looking at something on her phone as she walked.

A moment later, her head jerked up. "Oh!" She sidestepped at the last possible second, narrowly avoiding the collision. "Cambria?"

Blaine watched as the two women stood there, assessing each other.

Cambria bounced on the balls of her feet. A caramel-skinned beauty, she was tall, lean and leggy. Her long jet-black hair hung down her back, and her wide-legged denim jumper looked both comfortable and fashionable. "Eden?" It was more a squeal than a greeting. "I haven't seen you in ages!" She pulled her in for a hug.

"It's good to see you, Cambria." Eden returned the hug. "When did you get into town?"

"Like an hour ago. I promised Blaine I would come by the studio the next time I made it to town."

As the two friends stepped apart again, Eden's gaze drifted to meet his, and she narrowed her eyes just enough for him to see.

He frowned. *What's that about?*

"What?" Cambria tilted her head, her expression conveying confusion. Obviously, she'd noticed it, too.

"Nothing, nothing." She linked arms with Cambria, leading her away. "What brings you to town?"

He watched their retreating backs as they headed back toward the studio, chatting and giggling. He stood there a moment, trying to parse out what was going on. Eden seemed happy to see her friend, if a bit surprised. *So why did she cut her eyes at me like that?* He leaned against the wall, and as if on cue, Eden glanced back his way, a sour look on her face.

She did it again! Now I'm really confused. This was the thing about women that he didn't like. Their ever-changing emotions perplexed him. It seemed he often got into trouble with them but had no idea what he'd done wrong.

Not wanting to be on the receiving end of any more attitude from Eden, he shook his head and retreated back into the quiet of his office. There, he sat down at his desk, started up a Ludacris playlist on his phone and navigated to his email. He clicked through while bopping his head to the music, clearing out the clutter of unread messages and replying to those that required his attention. *I gotta stop letting my inbox get so out of hand.*

The music stopped, replaced by the sound of his ringtone. Swiping over the image of Marvin's business card on the screen, he answered the call. "Hi, Marvin. What's up?"

"Hey, Blaine. You doing all right? How's life in the Dirty South?"

He chuckled, as he always did whenever Marvin tried to sound hip. "It's all good, can't complain. But I'll be even better once you tell me what you thought of Naiya's album. It's amazing work, right?"

Marvin cleared his throat, remaining silent.

Blaine waited, leaning back in his chair and looking up at the ceiling. *He's hesitating...it's making me nervous.* But he didn't dare reveal that to his higher-up.

Marvin broke his silence. "This album is… Well, we know you worked super hard on it, with Naiya and Eden and the producers. And we absolutely think that 'The Way It Was,' 'Kisses at Dawn' and 'Look My Way' are absolutely fantastic tracks. Especially 'Look My Way.' How did you nail down Antoine 11 for that guest verse? He's pretty elusive these days."

Apparently, he's leading with the positive, so I'll just go with it for now. "Oh, a friend of mine knows one of Antoine's favorite producers. We hit him up, he hit up Antoine, and the rest is history, as they say. He's up in New York now, and since he couldn't make it down to the ATL, he just recorded his sixteen bars up there and we mixed it with Naiya's vocals after the fact."

"Awesome. Great job on securing the verse. It's a hot track, and everyone at Hamilton House agrees that having Antoine on the song will play very well with the fan base."

"Yeah, I agree. That's why we decided to approach him. It's sort of a hometown tag team, ya know? Antoine and a lot of that crew grew up in Atlanta. I think that's why he was so willing to work with Naiya, even though she's pretty new in the industry."

"Nice." He paused. "So, you're definitely on the right path with this album. However…"

Blaine frowned. *Here it comes.*

"...the other tracks on the album, are, well, not what we're looking for."

"Meaning? If you're going to say something like that about seventy percent of the album, I'd like to gain a little clarity here, Marvin."

He cleared his throat again. "Sure, sure. Absolutely. So, when we're looking at subject matter for the remainder of the album, you've got to admit the topics Naiya's singing about are pretty heavy."

Blaine rotated his chair so he could look out the window behind his desk. The gray sky and fat dark clouds indicated a coming storm. "That's a fair enough assessment, but that was done on purpose. What specifically do you have a problem with?"

"It's not me, Blaine. It's the team. I just want to be clear on that."

He flexed his jaw. "Then what is it that *the team* doesn't like?"

"Well... I mean...for instance, there are two songs about race stuff."

"You mean anti-Black bias?" Blaine gritted out.

Marvin coughed. "Yes, that. And then she's singing about how men are trash and rich whites are ruining the historically Black neighborhoods in Atlanta..."

He wanted to laugh but held back. "You mean misogyny and gentrification? Women do have to deal with a lot of crap from men on a daily basis, and gentrification is a problem in cities all over the country, not just in Atlanta." He paused, tapping his chin. *I can't pass up this chance to troll him a little.* "I've known you a long time, Marvin. And I know you're an intelligent, culturally aware person. You can't be telling me you're unfamiliar with these concepts."

Another series of coughs followed that.

Blaine tucked in his lower lip to hold back his chuckle.

"Yes, well, of course, I'm aware of these things," Marvin said once he got himself together. "Still, we don't think these are appropriate topics for Naiya's album. Especially not on a debut."

"Okay. And why is that?"

"You see, we want to put out music that counters the current toxic climate in media. You know, some positive vibes to cut through the negativity. We think Naiya's talents are well suited to the feel-good album of the year."

He shook his head. It was easy to see where this conversation was going. *I've got a choice here. I can cut my losses and agree with him now, or I can sit through twenty more minutes of corporate BS, just to end up with the same result.* "Level with me, Marvin. What does the team want us to do moving forward?"

"As I said, you're on the right path. We'd like you to keep the three standout tracks just as they are and revisit the creative process for the other tracks."

Blaine's mouth fell open for a moment. Snapping it shut, he asked, "Are you telling me we need to rework seven songs, seventy percent of this hard-won album, and rerecord them?"

"No, no. Of course not. What I'm saying is, just scrap the seven songs and start over. Build new songs, from the ground up."

He felt his jaw clench. "And is there another alternative here?"

"Not one that involves us funding the project." It was the bluntest statement Marvin had made for the entire conversation.

He blew out a breath. "I understand. Thanks for letting me know."

"I'm happy to help. Well, I'm due at a meeting soon. Have a good rest of your day, Blaine."

"You, too, Marvin." The words tasted like sour milk in his mouth, but he ground them out anyway. And moments later, he ended the call.

Shit.

Fifteen

A few minutes before nine Tuesday morning, Eden strolled through the open door of the small conference room at Against the Grain. The room, sparsely decorated with a few framed album covers, held only a few items. A mounted whiteboard took up one entire wall, and the opposite wall held only windows. Centered between the two walls, a rectangular table with seating for eight people took up most of the floor space.

She slipped into a seat on the side of the table closest to the door, tucking her purse into the chair next to her. She didn't think Blaine had any solid dress code for the meeting, so she'd kept it simple by wearing a silver silk blouse and wide-legged black slacks with her favorite low-heeled black leather loafers.

She'd been sitting there a minute or two, scrolling

through her phone, when Blaine strode in. He looked handsome as ever, wearing a pair of navy slacks; a button-down shirt featuring navy, hunter-green and white zigzags; and a pair of navy wingtips with a gold toe box. His locs were tied at his nape, and his favorite pair of dark sunglasses was perched atop his head.

Have mercy. Why does he have to be so fine? I could just stare at him all day. He always looked like a snack, no matter what he wore. But when she looked up at his face, she didn't see the mischievous smile she'd become accustomed to. Instead, she saw a guarded, taut expression that gave her pause. *Damn. What is he about to say?* She'd come into this meeting expecting to hear some good news about the album. Now that she'd seen his face, though, tiny needles of tension began to prick the base of her spine.

"Good morning, Eden." He greeted her as he took a seat at the end of the table to her right.

"Morning." She would have said more, but she was too busy worrying about what he might say.

She held his gaze for a second, and he winked at her.

"You all right down there, baby?"

She swallowed, knowing full well she wasn't okay. Because every time she looked at his handsome face, she felt her body temperature rise. "For now. I'm just... wondering what's about to happen, that's all."

Naiya breezed in a few moments later, clad in a floral sundress and flat nude sandals. Her wavy hair pulled back into a ponytail, she looked put together yet approachable.

Eden smiled and waved at Naiya, who waved back with a grin of her own.

Blaine cleared his throat. "Okay, ladies. Time to get down to business."

"Yes, let's," Naiya said, shifting from side to side in her seat. "What did the label team say about my album?"

Eden swallowed, bracing for whatever was about to spill from between the full lips that had kissed her senseless on more than one occasion.

He rested his elbows on the table, tenting his fingers. "I got some very positive feedback from Marvin. The team is especially fond of 'Look My Way'…"

Naiya grinned. "I knew they would be. That Antoine 11 verse is fire. I'm so glad he agreed to collab with me."

Eden nodded. "Yes. I mean when you combine his bars with Naiya's vocals…it's magic, really."

A slight smile tilted his lips. "I agree completely. The team also had a lot of great things to say about 'The Way It Was' and 'Kisses at Dawn.' Great work there as well, ladies."

She felt her brow crinkle. *He's said a lot of good things…about three out of ten tracks. What's he holding back here?* "Okay. This is all great to hear, but… I feel like you're leaving something out, Blaine."

"Yeah," Naiya interjected, running a hand over her hair. "Don't keep us in suspense. What was the feedback on the rest of the album?"

"Well…" He hesitated. Instead of saying more, he opened the leather portfolio. Taking out some documents, he slid copies to both of them. "In terms of feedback on the other seven tracks, I'd like you to take a look at this."

Eden scanned the top of the thin stack of papers, reading the headline on the first page. "'Official Correspondence. Hamilton House Recordings, a subsidiary of American Music Group Incorporated.'" Her eyes narrowed as she read further.

Naiya read along in silence, her lips flexing in time as her eyes perused the words on the page.

Eden got halfway down the first page before she saw a string of words that gave her pause. *Creative Revision Request.* Followed by another phrase that stopped her in her tracks. *Mandatory Change.* She looked up at Blaine, who avoided her gaze by pretending to look at the papers. *I'm sure he's already read them. That's probably why he can't look me in the eye.*

Naiya looked up, her eyes wide. "Blaine, what does all this mean? What are they asking us to do?"

He cleared his throat. "Well, Naiya, what the upper management team would like us to do is rework the seven remaining tracks on the album."

A few long, slow blinks later, Naiya said, "What?"

"Well, if you think about it, it's really a chance to dig deeper into your creative vision." He turned toward Eden. "The management team had its doubts about bringing you on for this project. But this allows you to keep your role as songwriter, as long as you're willing to make a few changes."

"Is it really, Blaine?" Eden, now reading through page three, held the document up as she read aloud. "'Clause C. Pursuant to the terms of this document, the following subject matter has been deemed "off-limits" for tracks on the album. Gentrification. Misogyny and Misogynoir. Rape Culture. Racism. Anti-Black Bias. Political affiliation'?" She dropped the papers on the desk. "That's only the first half of the list of things I'm not allowed to write about as lyricist, and that Naiya isn't allowed to sing about."

Naiya's mouth dropped open.

He held his hand out, open palm facing them. "Now, ladies. Think about how this could benefit album sales. We want to keep the subject matter light and…"

Naiya slowly shook her head, tears springing to her eyes. "No, Blaine. You told me that if I signed with you, you'd help me see my vision through to the end. You *promised* me."

He slumped, his head dropping to one side. "Don't you see, Naiya? That's exactly what I'm trying to do… deliver on that promise. I want to see your album in the hands of music lovers just as much as you do." He held up the document, flipping through the pages. "And to make that happen, all we have to do is sign on page five, agreeing to the terms that Hamilton House has set for us."

Eden closed her eyes, blew out a breath. "You don't even realize how you sound right now, do you?" She gestured to the crestfallen Naiya, who sat in stony silence, tears coursing down her cheeks. "Look at her, Blaine. She's a true talent. Passion. Stage presence. Vocal ability. And she actually has something meaningful to say."

"I agree, but—"

She held up her hand. "Let. Me. Finish. She has all those things going for her, and here you are trying to get her to go for the okey-doke. To record another cookie-cutter album, something that could be interchangeable with a thousand other female R & B albums. You're sitting here asking her to give up everything that makes her special." She looked over at the young singer. *I'd hug her if I thought it appropriate. She looks so sad.* "You've been here, you saw how hard we both worked on this. How could you, Blaine? How could you do that to her? To both of us?"

"Listen, I agree with everything you're saying. Naiya's talent, and her awareness of her surroundings, are so, so special. But Marvin is forcing my hand here. If we want to get this album out, we've got to make some sacrifices."

Naiya stood slowly, still shaking her head. "I…I can't do this."

Blaine stood, as well. "Naiya, wait. Let's talk about…"

"No." She dashed away her tears with her hand. "I'm leaving." Looking her way, she said, "Thank you, Eden. Thank you for seeing my vision."

Giving her a solemn nod, Eden watched as Naiya strode out the door. Then she looked at Blaine, not bothering to hide the hurt in her gaze. "I can't believe this is happening. I was so invested in this project… I feel like you're betraying me, all over again."

Left alone in the conference room with Eden, Blaine ran his hand over his eyes. *I haven't even gotten to the*

*heart of the document, and things have already gone
to the left in a major way.*

No, he hadn't expected that Naiya and Eden would be
thrilled about the prospect of all this extra work. But he
also hadn't thought they'd take the requests from Hamilton House as some kind of personal affront.

He shook his head. Upper management was accustomed to giving mandates and having them followed,
most of the time without questions or pushback. That
obviously wasn't going to happen in this instance, and
he knew they wouldn't like it. *I'm royally screwed here.*

"Did you even hear what I just said, Blaine?" Eden's
anger-laced voice cut through his thoughts like a chain
saw taking down a tree.

He looked her way and found her watching him, her
eyes narrowed, and her mouth twisted into a frown. He
gave a nervous little chuckle, hoping to soften her mood.
"Sorry, I checked out for a minute. What did you say?"

Her eyes narrowed further, indicating his attempt at
humor hadn't moved her. "I said, you haven't changed,
Blaine."

Leaning back in his chair, he held out his hands in
defense. "Whoa, whoa, whoa. This doesn't have anything to do with me being selfish or whatever. This is
simply business, Eden."

She scoffed, shaking her head. "Are you really that
thickheaded? You really think 'business' is the only
thing at play here?"

He felt his jaw tighten. The insinuation that he lacked
intelligence hit him in the gut like a punch. He'd heard
that all his life…even his own father chastised him for

leaning on his charm and good looks instead of using intelligence to get ahead. "Just because I can't read your mind or do some brainiac job in a lab somewhere, that doesn't mean I'm stupid."

"Blaine, I'm sorry. I'm not trying to insult your intelligence. I just need you to understand the stakes here."

"I didn't hear any complaints when we were making love."

She let her head drop back. "I can't. I can't with you."

"Maybe that's the problem here, Eden." He pushed his chair back from the table but stayed seated. "You can't open up to me. You've been talking about me being selfish, thoughtless and uncaring ever since you came here...yet you haven't told me why."

She sighed aloud, her fingertips rubbing her temples. "Why did I even come here? Why did I expect anything different from you?"

He shrugged, feeling his annoyance rising. "I don't know. You tell me."

She blew out a breath, pushed back from the table and stood. "You keep saying your hands are tied. That you don't have a choice. That it's all just 'business.' But none of that is true, Blaine. It's not true now, and it wasn't true seven years ago, either."

He threw up his hands. "Oh, boy. Here we go..."

"Hold up. I'm. Not. Finished."

He clamped his lips shut, though he wasn't thrilled about her tone or the direction she was taking the conversation.

"You made all these promises to Naiya. Told her you'd look out for her, make sure her album was true to her vision. Yet the very first time the suits in New York dispute what we worked so hard on you cave. Then you expect us to just go along with it."

He folded his arms over his chest but said nothing. *She's gone off and there's no need for me to speak. Anything I say right now will just be used against me.*

"Seven years ago, when the suits told you to disband Swatz Girlz you promised me a solo career. But when the label decided to ditch me and make Cambria a star, you caved then, too." She propped her fist on her hips, fixing him with an accusing stare. "Tell me, Blaine. How much pushback did you give them back then? Did you voice any opposition at all? Or did you just gleefully discard me like yesterday's trash?"

He cringed. "I think you're being unfair. These are two different situations."

She chuckled bitterly, with a slow shake of her head. "That's just it, Blaine. They aren't different, and I'll tell you why. You didn't stand up for Naiya." She looked away from him. "And you didn't stand up for me, either."

"Eden, I…"

"I don't want to hear it, Blaine. You keep acting as if I'm being unreasonable, as if it's all business and nothing personal. But in reality, it's very, very personal." She leaned over the table, placing her open palms on the tabletop. "You want to know why I don't fully trust you? Why I'm not open with you? Why I should never have let you into my bed or my heart?"

He swallowed.

"I'll tell you why. All the problems we've had, now

and in the past, can be traced back to one thing. Your absolute inability, or at least refusal, to stand up for someone else. To do what will be best for someone other than yourself."

He frowned. "That's a sweeping statement. I don't think it's accurate, either."

She scoffed.

"No, Eden. I'm not going to let you accuse me of being this callous jerk. I cared about you then, and I still care about you now. Whether you believe it or not, it's the truth."

"Fine." She slapped the table. "I'll make it more specific. You didn't stand up for Naiya. And it just serves to remind me of how you didn't stand up for me back in the day." She stood, her chin stuck out defiantly. "I can't do this with you, Blaine. I won't."

"You won't what? Make changes to the album?"

"Ugh." She sounded disgusted. "Fuck those guys at Hamilton House. I don't care about their demands or their stupid contracts. And as for you and me, it's over. I'm not going to keep being involved with someone who doesn't have my back when it really counts."

"What about us? What about everything we've shared?"

"I'm not gonna deny the connection we share, Blaine. But I have to be careful when it comes to my heart. I can't risk the pain of having you betray me again."

That stung, and he felt his heart clench. "I care about you. I feel like…like we have something special between us."

"Bullshit. I don't want to hear declarations like that

when it's so obvious you're not going to do anything to prove it."

He stood and walked around to where she was. Grasping her arm, he pulled her toward him, letting his lips crash against hers. For a few fiery moments, she leaned into him, their tongues tangling like the ball of emotions rolling around in his stomach.

Then she snatched herself away from him. Her expression was strained, tortured. "Don't, Blaine."

"Eden, you can't just walk out like this."

"Watch me." Shooting him one last hard, cutting look, she snatched up her purse, turned her back and strode out of the room. Her echoing footsteps sounded on the concrete floor as she retreated, moving farther and farther away by the second.

Alone in the room, he rested his elbows on the table and dropped his head in his hands.

Sixteen

Stretched out on the sofa in sweatpants and an old tee, Eden flipped absently through the pages of one of her fashion magazines. The flat-screen television, tuned to one of those home renovations shows, provided little more than background noise. And while the house was quiet for now, she knew Cooper and Ainsley were due home soon from his baseball practice.

It was Wednesday evening, the middle of what seemed like the longest week of her life. This time last week she'd been on a high. She and Blaine had been making sweet love and creating music together, and Naiya's project had been on the cusp of wrapping up.

Now everything had crashed down around her. *I always sucked at Jenga. Always pulling the wrong block, or not keeping my hand steady enough. Now my life is scattered just like those wooden blocks.*

She let her head drop back against the cushion, staring at the ceiling. She knew how cliché it was for her to be lying here like this, pining over a man who'd shown himself to be unreliable on more than one occasion. Yet she couldn't shake the feeling. Because there was more to him. There was a sweet, loving side to him…a man who held doors and pulled out chairs, whose smile lit up a room, who made love to her like a champion. And knowing all the goodness inside him only made this situation harder to take. All she wanted to do was lie there, like a bump on a pickle, kicking herself for getting involved with Blaine in the first place.

She heard the front door open and turned her head.

Ainsley entered, her arms laden with grocery bags. Cooper came in right behind her.

"Hey, Auntie," he shouted as he shut the door behind them.

"Hey, Coop." She sat up on the couch, righting her disheveled clothing a bit. "How was practice?"

"Good. I got to work on pitching today." He jogged past her, setting a paper grocery bag on the counter in the kitchen before returning. "Coach says I've got a pretty good arm."

"Of course, you do." She flexed her biceps. "It's in your genes, kiddo."

He laughed. "Auntie." Shaking his head, he disappeared up the stairs.

Ainsley, who'd muscled her bags into the kitchen, stood in the doorway, shaking her head. "You two.

Meanwhile, why don't you get up and help me put these groceries away? Obviously, Cooper has a more pressing engagement with *Minecraft*."

Eden frowned. "I guess I should. I've probably been vegging on the couch way too long." She stood, stretching her arms above her head.

Ainsley cocked a brow. "Girl, what's going on with you? You didn't come home from the studio yesterday, then I come home today and find you here, leaving an Eden-sized divot in the sofa. This ain't like you, E."

She shook her head as she entered the kitchen. "You're telling me." As she and Ainsley plucked items from the bags sitting on the counter and the island, tucking them into their designated spots, she related the story of what had happened during yesterday's meeting at Against the Grain.

"But where'd you go after that?" Ainsley hung a bunch of bananas on the little silver hook stand she kept on the counter solely for that purpose. "Why didn't you come home last night?"

She shrugged. "I just… I don't know. My emotions were high, and I wanted to be alone. So, when I left the studio, I called Naiya to apologize to her. Even though it's not my fault, I know what she's going through, and I sympathize."

Ainsley nodded.

"Then I headed down to the park. Sat on the dock by the lake for hours, then checked into a hotel when it started to get dark. I couldn't come home. I couldn't face you and Cooper knowing how angry and hurt I was. I would never want to take it out on the two of you, my only real family."

Ainsley made a face. "Oh, damn. I'm sorry, girl."

"Yeah. I feel like hell. No appetite, can't sleep." She dropped her gaze. "That's on top of feeling like Boo Boo the Fool."

"No, I mean, I'm sorry you felt you couldn't come home." She placed her hand atop Eden's. "We love you no matter what. We love you at your best and at your worst. I'm just upset you suffered alone."

Eden felt the smile creep over her face, despite her mood. "Thank you, Ainsley. I really appreciate that."

"And if you want me to go over there and kick Blaine's ass, just let me know." She balled up her fists and positioned herself in a fighting stance. "I've got a clean record; I probably won't get in too much trouble for putting him in traction."

She giggled. "You're the best."

Ainsley chuckled, too. "Guess what I brought home from the store, cousin?"

"What?"

"Triple fudge brownie ice cream. Nuts. Whipped cream." She extracted each item from a bag as she called them out. "You down for a sundae?"

"Do you really have to ask?"

A few minutes later, they were both on the couch with their bowls and spoons.

"So, what are you going to do about Blaine?"

She shrugged. "Go back to what I was doing before, I guess. Pretend he doesn't exist."

"What about Naiya's album?"

"I held up my end of the deal. I wrote ten solid songs, based on her own words and feelings. I got paid for my work."

Ainsley scoffed. "Yeah, yeah. We both know you ain't gonna leave that girl hanging. She could have been me back in the day. Or you." She gave her a pointed look.

She sighed. "You're right. I definitely see my younger, more idealistic self in her. I'd hate for her to give up or change herself to try to fit into the industry." She scratched her chin. "I'll reach out to her in a few days, see what she wants to do moving forward."

"Fair enough." Ainsley set her empty bowl on the coffee table. "Now, about Blaine…"

She shook her head. "No. I don't want to talk about him."

"Eden, you're not going to be able to forget him or pretend he doesn't exist, and you know I'm right." She touched her shoulder. "You're just not that kind of person. You're going to care about him no matter what."

The last spoonful of ice cream lost some of its chocolaty flavor when she heard those words. "Damn it, Ainsley. Stop telling me the truth and tell me what will make me feel better."

"Girl, stop whining. You know I'm all about keeping it one hundred." Settling back against the cushion, she tossed one leg over the other. "Here's what's real. You love him. And even though you're mad at him, and rightfully so, that's not gonna negate your feelings for him. You are gonna have to figure out a way to make it work."

"Ugh." She ran a hand through her messy hair. "That was physically painful to hear."

"Like our queen, Lizzo, said, truth hurts." Ainsley shrugged. "So are you gonna call him or what? Odds are he's just as miserable as you are."

She shook her head. "No way. After what he did, he'll have to call me." She wasn't about to let him off easy, not after he'd given her a repeat performance of his self-centered ways. As badly as she wanted to call him, if only to hear his voice, she knew she couldn't do it. She'd simply have to set her intense longing for him aside...as best she could, anyway.

"All right, I guess that'll do." Ainsley wrinkled her nose, the way she did when in deep thought. "I know he's gonna call you. It might take him some time to get his head out of his ass, though."

"Whatever." Eden yawned. "I'm tired of talking about him."

Grabbing the remote, Ainsley searched through the on-screen guide. "Looks like *Idlewild* is coming on."

Eden chuckled, then settled in for her fiftieth viewing of her cousin's favorite film.

Thursday night, Blaine reclined in the engineer's chair in the soundboard suite of his studio. The room, darkened except for the electronic glow emitted by the controls, matched his mood. His very soul felt shrouded in black, and the few points of light he could see all pointed back to one thing.

Eden.

No one had been in the studio since Monday, as no

one had booked studio time this week. He'd asked his receptionist to leave the schedule open, just in case work on Naiya's album took longer than expected. He only had one studio in his building, though he dreamed of one day building a state-of-the-art facility with at least three recording suites.

For now, though, all the dreams he held dear faded into the background, overshadowed by the immense pain of Eden's absence from his life. He'd tried calling and texting her all day and into the night Tuesday; she'd ignored every attempt. By Wednesday morning, he'd given up on getting back into her good graces. Then he'd trudged here, to his big empty workplace, come into the studio and plugged in his headphones to hear the one sound he craved more than any other.

Blaine had not left the studio last night; he'd only left the room to go to the bathroom or grab the occasional beverage. His appetite was nonexistent, and he hadn't eaten a substantial meal in the last thirty-six hours. Still, he didn't want to leave, didn't want to set his headphones aside.

I want to be here, where she was. I need to be near where this began, where I can still feel her energy.

He leaned the chair back as far as it would go without unplugging his headphones. Stretched his stiff legs out in front of him. Focused only on the sweet, sweet sound filling his ears. Music always salved the wounds of his soul…this time was no different.

The door of the soundboard suite swung open, and the motion in his periphery made him jerk his head in that direction. He could make out a figure in the dim light but couldn't yet see the man's face. He rubbed his tired eyes, but that didn't help. Straightening up in the chair, he called out, "Who's there?"

The lights flickered on, and he closed his eyes against the brightness. He looked again, seeing his brother through his bleary eyes. Gage's mouth was moving, but he couldn't make out the words over the sound playing in his headphones.

Gage stalked closer, his expression decidedly annoyed. "Can't you hear me?" He shouted the question.

"Yeah, how could I not when you're yelling."

Shaking his head, Gage demanded, "Take off those damn headphones so I can talk to you!"

He simply shook his head. *Whatever Gage wants to talk about, it can't possibly sound better to me than what I'm listening to.*

Gage narrowed his eyes, and after a few moments of searching for the jack, he snatched the headphone cord out of place. "There. Since you wanna be a stubborn ass." He paused, his gaze shifting to the soundboard as the sounds poured into the room. "What are you listening to?" He frowned, tapping his chin with his index finger for a few seconds. "Wait. Isn't this Eden singing?"

He nodded slowly. "I just…needed to hear her voice."

"Wow. You're mighty pitiful right now, bro."

"You're right, and I'm aware of it." He resisted the urge to shush his brother, whose idle chatter was interrupting his listening to the sweet sounds of Eden's melodic crooning.

"This is that Lauryn Hill song." He shifted his weight from one foot to the other. "'The Sweetest Thing.'"

"Yep. It's one of her favorite songs, and she recorded this as a warm-up before she started recording studio demos for Naiya to use."

He gazed off to the side, the way he always did when trying to remember something. "I remember this...it was on that soundtrack to that Black nineties chick flick...what was it? *The Inkwell? Jason's Lyric?*"

"Love Jones." He swallowed the lump of pain in his throat. "Don't make me have to revoke your Black card."

Shaking his head, Gage stepped closer to him before stopping and wrinkling his nose. "When's the last time you went home to...you know, shower?"

He shrugged. "Tuesday."

Moving over to the soundboard, Gage shut off the playback. "Nope. That's not going to be acceptable, buddy." He grabbed his brother's hand and pulled him from the chair. "Get up. We're going to your house."

He felt his pulse quicken, the absence of Eden's angelic voice already starting to affect him. Listening to her isolated vocals while picturing her beautiful smile was the only thing that gave him comfort as of late. "I don't want to leave."

"I get that. But if you ever want another shot at someone as classy as Eden, you're gonna have to get off your ass." With one strong tug, Gage moved him toward the door. "Let's go."

"She's not going to talk to me. I tried calling, texting." He felt the pain in his chest, the same pain he felt every time he remembered the look of hurt on her face. "She just ignored me."

"I would, too. What are we, twelve? Grown-ass adults settle their disputes face-to-face." Gage wrinkled his nose again. "You'll see her in person. *After* you bathe, because you funky as hell."

"Stop roasting me, Gage. I'm already in pain."

He dropped his hand. "Whatever. Do you love her or not? And don't even think about lying to me, bruh. Mama already hipped me to the game."

He sighed. "Yes, Gage. I love her." Before she reentered his life, he'd resolved that love wasn't for him. It was simply a youthful feeling, something he'd grown too old and too business-minded to entertain. Now he knew better. Because there was no way he could deny her ownership of his heart and soul.

Gage clapped his hands together. "Sho' you right. Now, man up, get your shit together and go get your woman!"

He didn't put up a fight. He knew his brother was right, though he'd never say it aloud. But how would he convince her to let him back into her heart, when she wouldn't even answer his calls?

What will I have to do to get her to see me?

Whatever it was, he'd have to figure it out. Because the past few days had taught him something, an undeniable truth.

He didn't want to live this life without her in it.

Seventeen

Friday afternoon, Eden and Ainsley sat at the dining room table, enjoying burgers from the Slutty Vegan, Atlanta's premiere vegan burger joint. The silence in the room was broken when Eden's phone started ringing.

"Whew." Eden swiped her mouth with a napkin. "I need a time-out."

Sliding the button on her screen, she answered the call from the 212-area code. "Hello?"

"Hi, I'm looking for Eden Voss?" The female voice on the other line seemed hesitant.

"That's me. What can I do for you?"

"Oh, good. Hi, Ms. Voss. My name is Chanel Titus—but most people call me…"

Eden's eyes widened as she completed her sentence. "Chanel The Titan?"

Chanel giggled. "Yes. Apparently, you're familiar with my work."

"I am. You've worked with some of the biggest names in hip-hop and R & B. Monica. Sevyn. Riri... the list goes on."

"I'm flattered that you follow my career." Chanel cleared her throat. "Listen, the reason I'm contacting you is that I was in the Hamilton House offices here in New York last week for a meeting. While I was there, I overheard a voice singing on a demo reel. I was so taken aback by the talent that I inquired, and as it turns out, the voice I heard was yours."

Eden felt the rush of exhilaration as the heat rose into her cheeks. "Wow. Oh, wow. Thank you so much."

"I looked you up online, and realized I'd already heard some of the songs you've written. But you haven't put out any music of your own. Why is that?"

She clutched the phone, her eyes darting to Ainsley, who could hear the whole conversation.

"Tell her," Ainsley insisted.

So, she gave Chanel the short version of her only attempt at a singing career. "I've just sort of settled into the behind-the-scenes work of songwriting, which I love."

"Well, honey, you can keep writing songs if you like. But you're wasting your vocal talents by not using them." She paused. "Listen, I'll level with you. I'd love to work with you on an album. You've got the kind of voice R & B is missing right now."

"An album?" She blinked several times. "I...just... wow, my own album?"

"If you'd rather start with just a single, to see how things go, I'm open to that." Chanel said something to someone in the background, her speech muffled as if she'd placed her hand over the microphone. "Okay, honey. I've got another meeting. You have my number now, so if you decide to give it a shot, just give me a call."

"Sure thing. Thanks so much." Ending the call, she laid her phone face down on the table.

Ainsley squealed. "Giiirlll! Chanel the Titan wants to work with you!"

She took a deep breath, blowing it out through her lips. "I know. This is wild."

"It gets wilder if you think about it."

She frowned. "What do you mean?"

"In a roundabout way, Blaine helped you get Chanel's attention."

Her frown deepened.

"No, listen. If you hadn't agreed to work with him, what are the odds you'd have recorded that particular demo, which ended up in the Hamilton House office, at that particular time, for Chanel to hear it?"

She felt her face relax. "I guess…if you look at it that way, Blaine played a small part in this."

"No ma'am. Blaine played a big part in this. Give that man his credit." Ainsley went back to devouring her burger.

She leaned back in her chair. "At least something good came of me getting my heart stepped on by Blaine Woodson for the second time in a decade."

"I'm just glad you're not going to turn down the opportunity." Ainsley dabbed the Slutty Sauce from her mouth with a napkin. "And I want you to be open to other opportunities that come your way too, E."

"Like what? I don't have much else going on right now."

"You could. My dating sense is tingling."

"Ugh." She threw up her hands. "The last thing I need in my life right now is a new man."

"You're absolutely right." She stood, stuffing her trash into the paper sack. "Lucky for you, I'm not talking about a new man. I'm talking about Blaine."

"Come on, Ainsley. I told you I'm not going to call him."

"I haven't forgotten what you said. Don't worry. He's going to reach out." She put their trash into the can, then grabbed a sponge to wipe down the table. "And when he does, you're going to give him a chance this time, right?"

She frowned.

"Promise me, Eden. Promise me you'll at least hear him out."

"And if I still think he's full of shit after he's said his piece, then what?" She folded her arms over her chest.

"Then you're free to tell him to kick rocks in flip-flops. I'm not demanding an outcome. I'm just asking you to give the brotha a shot."

"Fine." She wasn't particularly happy about Ainsley's harping, but she knew her cousin. It'd be much easier to say yes now than be badgered about it for days on end. "You get on my last nerve, Ainsley."

"I love you, too, cousin." Blowing her a kiss, Ainsley slipped from the room, leaving her alone at the table.

When Blaine rapped on the door of his father's hobby room Saturday morning, he had no idea what to expect. Knocks on this door often went ignored if his father was busy building or painting one of the hundreds of model military aircraft and vehicles he'd collected over the years, or reading up on military history. Aside from that, Blaine himself hadn't set foot inside the hobby room since his days as a rebellious teen.

Clutching the handles of the large paper shopping bag, he waited a few moments. He could hear his father's movements inside the room. He knocked again, in case his first one had gone unheard.

Caleb snatched the door open this time. He wore an old tee, blue sweatpants and the canvas apron he wore when at work on his hobby. He frowned. "Blaine? What are you doing here, son?"

He took a deep breath. "We need to talk, Dad, and it's a long-overdue conversation."

Caleb's frown deepened. "Not now, Blaine. I'm working on…"

He held up the bag. "Dad, I hate to interrupt you. But I brought something I know you'll want."

His father's gaze flickered to the nondescript brown bag, then back to his son's face. "What could possibly be in there that I'd want?"

"How about two perfect 1/144-scale model kits for the Blue Angels Aerobatic Team aircraft?"

Confusion knit his brow. "Are you serious?"

He shook the bag gently, hearing the pieces inside rustling and rattling around. "Take a look for yourself."

Taking the offered bag from his son's hand, Caleb peered inside. His eyes widened when he saw the contents. He immediately stepped back from the doorway. "Come on in."

Blaine smiled as he entered his father's sacred space for the first time in a decade. The room hadn't changed much in configuration over the years. There was a brown leather love seat and a coffee table to one side. His father's workstation, a huge, custom-built oak table, was littered with paints, brushes and model parts, sectioned off with the four raised dividers built into the tabletop. The table's unique design made it possible for Caleb to work on several models at one time without getting the pieces mixed up.

"Have a seat, Blaine." Caleb sat down on the love seat, already taking the brightly colored, shrink-wrapped boxes out of the bag.

"Thanks." Taking up the seat next to his father, he settled in. He watched quietly as his father inspected the two packages, the spark of interest glowing in his dark eyes.

"Where did you find these?"

"Online. I remember how much you loved Blue Angels memorabilia, and after consulting with Mom, I found out what was missing from your collection." He flexed his fingers. "Took a bit of digging, but I found them. I'd say I learned a decent amount while searching for the models." He leaned back. "Why don't you quiz me?"

Caleb chuckled, a rare sound indeed. "All right. What do you know about the Blue Angels?"

"Cool. The Blue Angels are the United States Navy's flight demonstration squadron, formed in 1946. That makes them the world's second-oldest aerobatics team. The squadron had two headquarters, one at Naval Base Pensacola in Florida, and the other at Naval Base El Centro in California."

Caleb appeared impressed. "I see you've done some research. Now, what can you tell me about the aircraft you brought?"

"I've got two models, the Lockheed Hercules C-130, and the McDonnell-Douglas F4-J Phantom II. The C-130 was developed in the 1950s and has been used ever since by the US Air Force for tactical transport, parachute drops of personnel and equipment, and air mission landing. This particular model has been used to transport the Angels since 1970."

Tilting his head slightly, Caleb said, "Go on."

Blaine felt the connection growing between them, so he continued. "As for the Phantom II, it's one of several models of jets used to provide escort and support to the squadron during aerobatics demonstrations. This particular model was in use by the Angels from 1969 to 1974—the Vietnam era."

Caleb blinked several times. His shoulders relaxed, releasing the rigidity that always seemed to reside there, and he released a slow breath. "Wow, son. I'm...pleasantly surprised."

"It gets better, Dad." He rubbed his hands together, noticing they weren't sweaty the way they usually were when he was in his father's presence. Talking with him about the models seemed to have put them both at ease. "I got all the manufacturer recommended paints as well, and I want to spend today helping you put them together."

Caleb's eyes grew wet. "Really?"

He nodded. "Yes. I figure you can work on the C-130, and I'll do the jet since it's smaller and I don't know what the hell I'm doing."

He laughed, a deep, rumbling sound Blaine hadn't heard in years. "Sounds wonderful. I just so happen to have a couple of slots open on my table that we can use." He put the boxes back in the bag and set it on the floor near his feet.

"Great." He grabbed his father's hand. "Before we get started, though, I want to begin with an apology."

"I'm listening, son." His voice was soft, welcoming, not gruff and irritated.

"I've been so stubborn. I've locked myself away from you and the rest of the family, trying to prove I could do things on my own. For a long time, I relished being the 'black sheep,' thinking that made me daring and independent." He sighed. "But these last few years, even the last few weeks, have shown me the value of relationships with people you love." A vision of Eden's radiant smile passed through his mind, and he cringed at the pain that clenched his chest whenever he thought of her. "I'm ready to try to put this relationship back together, Dad. And I know that begins with me saying I'm sorry."

Caleb gave his hand a squeeze. "I accept your apology, son. But I also admit my part in this. You inherited that stubbornness from me, truth be told." He shook his head, chuckling wryly. "I've been too hard on you. For years, I tried to force you to be someone you're not, just because I thought I knew what was best for you." He looked past Blaine as if seeing something beyond him. "I've been thinking a lot lately about an old friend, someone I lost years ago. He has a son, too. About your age. But the difference is, my friend died." He looked back to Blaine. "He's not here to love and guide his son, to share moments like this with him. Knowing that…makes me so grateful I get the chance to tell you I'm sorry."

Caleb tugged his hand, and Blaine let himself be enveloped by his father's embrace. Several long moments passed with them holding each other, and Blaine smiled. He could see the young boy who lived inside him, who longed for closeness with his dad, smiling as well.

When they parted, Caleb said, "I've got to know… what brought this on?"

Blaine's smile faded. "Actually, it was Eden. She asked why we weren't on good terms and said I should reach out."

Caleb nodded. "Tell her I said thank you."

He shook his head. "I would…but I don't think she'll speak to me." He proceeded to give his father a quick rundown of what had transpired between them.

When he finished, Caleb gave him that stern, fatherly look. "You realize she's right, don't you? It really was your own stubbornness that landed you in this situation."

He sighed. "Yes, Dad. I know she's right, and I'm wrong."

"Well, if I were you, I'd figure out a way to tell her that. A woman like Eden is rare, and second chances with someone like her are probably one in a million." He stood, stretched. "Tell you what. We'll figure something out while we put these models together."

Eighteen

Sitting beneath an umbrella on a grassy lawn at Piedmont Park, Eden watched her nephew running and playing with his friends.

Ainsley sat next to her on the outdoor blanket, grinning as they looked on. "Look at him. You'd never know he was injured, the way he's getting around now. I'm glad we went ahead with that surgery."

She nodded. "Me, too. He's been so happy ever since he started playing baseball." She smiled, watching him turn a cartwheel. "It was expensive but totally worth it." Seeing Cooper so happy melted her heart.

"They've been running like that for a solid hour," Ainsley remarked. "Do you think they've overdosed on sugar?"

Eden snorted. "Girl, please. Of course, they have!

We brought seven ten- to twelve-year-olds out here, and fed them a cake, ice cream, cookies and punch." She shook her head as one girl leapfrogged over a boy's back. "We're lucky if they don't start levitating."

Ainsley fell out laughing.

"It's a good thing we brought them to the park. They need the space to run and jump and burn off all that sugar, anyway." Eden giggled.

Cooper ran over to where they sat. He was quite a sight, his blue T-shirt and shorts covered in grass stains, orange frosting and drips of vanilla ice cream. His conical birthday hat sat cocked at an odd angle on his head, just barely clinging on.

"Look at that hat, Coop." She gave her nephew a fist bump. "You're an expert level hat-bender."

He laughed, reaching up to adjust it. Smiling brightly, he said, "Mom, Aunt Eden, thanks a lot. This is my best birthday ever!" He knelt briefly to gift them hugs and kisses, and then he was off again, blazing across the grass to rejoin his friends.

"Is it just me, or did he leave a trail of exhaust behind him?" Eden grinned.

Ainsley shook her head, brushing away at the tears gathering in her eyes. "I can't believe my baby is eleven whole years old. Seems like yesterday he was just learning to walk."

"You can always have another one," she chided, elbowing her playfully.

Rolling her eyes, Ainsley countered, "Not on your life. Cooper keeps me plenty busy. Besides, I'd need a man for that, and I'm fresh out of prospects for the time being."

"Not really," Eden teased. "What about Gage?"

"Whatever. He's my boss."

Eden shrugged. "So what? Are you saying people who work together can't have a romance?"

"Obviously that's not the case. Look what happened between you and Blaine." The moment the words came out, Ainsley clamped her hand over her lips. "I'm sorry, girl. I didn't mean to bring him up."

"It's okay. I know you just want to change the subject from you and Gage."

Ainsley punched her cousin playfully in the shoulder, then returned to her reclining position.

Silence fell between them for a few moments, and Eden returned to watching the kids play. Several were involved in a fierce game of Frisbee, while the others crowded around one of Cooper's gifts, an insect guidebook and collection kit.

As she looked on, she felt a little spark of something deep inside. The part of her that wanted to one day mother a child, whether a smart, thrill-seeking son like Cooper or a little girl with a sharp mind and the fierce determination she'd inherited from her mother. She only wanted one child, whom she'd probably spoil and dote on endlessly. But as the years passed, she'd settled into accepting that maybe a child wasn't in the cards for her. If that were the case, she'd be content to continue playing the role of World's Greatest Aunt for Cooper.

Or at least that's what she told herself.

Blaine's face appeared in her mind. She didn't push

the thought away this time, allowing herself the fantasy for a few moments. What if he weren't selfish? What if he stood up for her when she needed him, but wasn't afraid to tell her when she was out of pocket? What if he wanted to build a life with her and be there to help raise that precious child she wanted so badly? But he was loving, an inner voice reminded her. He was caring, and kind, and had more drive to succeed than most. She knew she and this hypothetical child would always be loved and well cared for, because Blaine wouldn't have it any other way.

She dwelt on those thoughts for so long, she started to hear his voice, calling her name.

Then Ainsley's voice joined Blaine's.

Confused, she returned to reality. Turning to Ainsley, she saw her pointing across the field, toward the park entrance.

And when she looked, she saw Blaine, striding in her direction.

He wore a pair of tan jeans, a bright yellow button-down shirt printed with palm trees, and pristine white sneakers. He carried a huge bag emblazoned with multicolored balloons in one hand and had a bouquet of yellow roses and marigolds cradled beneath his opposite arm. With those signature dark sunglasses over his eyes, his locs flowing freely around his shoulders, he was a vision of casually dressed handsomeness.

She swallowed. "What's he doing here? How did he know where I was?"

Ainsley winked. "Oh. Did I forget to tell you I invited him to Cooper's birthday party?" She climbed to her feet.

Standing up herself, Eden did her best to smooth the wrinkles out of her lavender tunic and knock off the blades of grass clinging to her purple leggings. "Ainsley, I'm gonna hide your favorite lace-front for this."

"Don't you dare touch Tanisha!" Ainsley cut her a threatening look. "That wig set me back a pretty penny. The lace is invisible, I tell you. *Completely invisible.*" She gestured toward Blaine, whose long strides were quickly closing the distance. "Look at the size of that bag! Whatever's in there is bound to be a pretty sweet gift for your nephew."

"Whatever." She slid her feet into the jeweled flip-flops she'd worn to the park. "I'm gonna deal with you later, trust and believe." She swallowed again, doing her best to get herself together.

Because in a few more steps, Blaine Woodson would be in her personal space.

As he moved across the grass toward where Eden sat with Ainsley, Blaine ran through what he'd planned to say in his mind.

Eden, you were right. I should have stood up for you. I'm sorry I didn't make you feel safe and cared for.

If you'll let me make it up to you, I promise it'll be worth it.

He kept a tight grip on the handles of the bag and the flowers, partly because of nerves, and partly to make sure his gifts reached their recipients undamaged. He'd brought something for the birthday boy, of course, but he'd also brought a small gift for his mother.

If it hadn't been for Ainsley inviting me here, I don't know how I would have convinced Eden to see me.

He saw them stand up and could see their mouths moving but still wasn't close enough to hear what they were saying to each other. Piedmont Park was an expansive green space, so getting to them through the gaggles of folks who'd come out to enjoy the mild temperatures and sunny weather of this early September Sunday would take some time.

He could make out the expression on Eden's beautiful face, and it seemed somewhere between surprise and confusion. *I'm guessing Ainsley invited me but didn't tell Eden.*

As he came to the edge of their blanket, he stopped. Smiling, he handed the bag over to Ainsley. "Hey, Ainsley. Thanks for the invite—I put a little something for you in with Cooper's gift."

"Much obliged, Blaine. Thanks for coming."

His gaze slid to Eden. Casually dressed in a two-tone purple outfit, she still looked as beautiful as any runway model to his eyes.

Ainsley giggled. "I'll…just take this over to Cooper. You two go ahead and chat." Still giggling, she walked away with the gift bag.

"Hi, Eden." He didn't move closer, unsure he'd be able to resist the urge to pull her into his arms.

"Hi, Blaine." She blushed slightly, giving him a side-long glance. "Thanks for bringing Cooper a birthday gift."

"Of course." He shifted his weight from left to right and back. "I'm afraid I'm not up on what eleven-year-olds are into these days, so I consulted my little cousin Jack. Hopefully, he likes what I got him."

She gave him the smallest smile. "I'm sure he'll love it. I appreciate you doing your research."

He remembered the flowers tucked under his arm and inched just close enough to offer them to her. "Ainsley said these are your favorite flowers. I hope you like them." He genuinely did, since he felt like a fourteen-year-old, cozying up to his crush.

She took the flowers, bringing them to her face for a sniff. "They're beautiful." She gestured to the blanket. "Do you want to…sit down? Chat for a minute?"

"I'll stay as long as you'll let me."

She nodded, then took a graceful seat while balancing the flowers in her hands.

He joined her, leaving a respectable distance between them. He couldn't help remembering that the last time they were on this blanket, she'd been sitting atop his lap, and they'd been kissing passionately. His groin tightened in response to the memory. He knew better than to lead with that, though. "Before I start, I just want to pass on a message from my father. He said to tell you thanks."

Her brow crinkled. "What? Why?"

"Because of your harping…"

She poked him with her index finger. "Watch it, Blaine."

He chuckled. "I meant, because of your *encouragement*, I tried to connect with him. I reached out to him with something he's passionate about and used that to tear down the wall between us."

"Really?"

"Yes. And aside from that, Dad's willing to offer financing for Naiya's album, if I need it. We're on good terms now, and I'm grateful to have his support. I'm glad I took your advice, Eden."

She smiled, soft and lovely. "That's great. But...I can't take credit for that."

"Sure, you can. No one else has ever been able to get through to me when it came to my dad. And trust me, plenty of people have tried." His siblings, his friends, even Trevor, his engineer, had brought it up on several occasions. But no one had been able to move the needle...until Eden. "You're magical, Eden. That's the only explanation I have. I can't tell you how good it feels, after all these years, to be on such good terms with my father."

Her smile broadened. "Wow. That's amazingly sweet of you to say."

"It's true. Every word." He reached out. "Can I... hold your hand for a minute?" He missed the feel of her satin skin against his. And while he didn't expect her to open up to him, he'd take whatever she'd give him.

She nodded.

He enfolded her hand in his own. The words he'd planned to say swirled around in his mind, the imagery as bold as a Hype Williams music video. Yet when he opened his mouth, only four words spilled out. "Eden, I love you."

She gasped. "Blaine, you..."

He squeezed her hand. "Please, let me get this out before I lose my nerve. I'm a fool for not telling you how I felt earlier. And an even bigger ass for not showing you." He looked into the golden-brown orbs of her eyes, seeing the emotion there, silently praying that her feelings matched his own. Yet whatever she decided, he'd accept it. "You were right. Everything you said about me was true. I was being selfish, putting my own desire for success above your feelings, your career. I'm so, so sorry for what I've done. I know I can't go back and change any of it, but I hope you'll accept my sincere apology."

Her mouth hung open.

"And I don't want you to think I'm not going to do something about Naiya's album. I'm not sure what just yet. But we've all worked too hard to let it end like this."

Tears sprang to her eyes, her lips trembling.

He stiffened. "Oh, no. Did I say something wrong? Have I hurt you again?" He'd never forgive himself if he caused her even one more moment of pain. She'd already suffered enough because of him.

She shook her head. "No, you haven't hurt me." She moved closer to him. "You've made me so very happy." She showed him a watery smile before placing a soft kiss on his cheek. "And I applaud your patience. I know I've come across pretty judgmental...rigid...immovable."

He feigned confusion. "What? I hadn't noticed."

She giggled. "Do you have any idea how long I've been waiting for you to come around, you knucklehead?"

He laughed. "Close to a decade, I'm guessing."

"You'd be right." She clamped her soft hands around

his face, tilting it until their gazes met. "I'm glad you love me, Blaine Woodson. Because I love you, too."

His heart swelled, warmth flooding his body like he'd taken a shot of brown liquor. Only his beautiful, caring Eden was far more intoxicating than even the finest aged bourbon. "You can't imagine how relieved and grateful I am to hear you say that."

"Why don't you kiss me and show me?" She dragged her fingertip over his lips.

With a groan, he pulled her in and kissed her, long and slow. His arms wrapped around her body, and she leaned in, pressing herself against him. His tongue stroked, hers teased, and before long, he'd forgotten where he was.

It was only a chorus of *"Eeeww!"* coming from several young voices that pulled them apart a few moments later.

"Sorry. I forgot about the young eyes watching." He gave her a sheepish grin.

"Hey! What kind of party you two think this is?" Ainsley shouted the words at them from a few feet away, in a voice laced with humor.

Shaking her head, Eden put her hands to her face, covering the deep red tinge of her cheeks. "I think we'd better put off the rest of that for later."

"I agree. Because what I plan on doing to you is definitely not G-rated." He winked.

She tossed her curly head back and laughed, and it was the most beautiful sound he'd ever heard.

Nineteen

Eden walked through the halls of Marian Gardens Retirement Home Tuesday morning, her steps measured and slow. Most of the rooms she passed had their doors shut, but she'd occasionally see an elderly woman or man inside their room. Some were asleep or being visited by nurses or other care providers. A few were up sitting in their recliners and made eye contact with her as she walked by. She offered a smile and wave but kept moving. She wasn't exactly comfortable in a place like this, probably due to her limited experience. Still, she'd come here for something important, and she'd already put it off too long. Her time to take care of it might well be running out.

Taking the elevator, then navigating another long

hallway, she finally came to the room the nurse at the front desk had sent her to. 4L.

His name was printed on a small plaque hanging on the door, and she silently read it. *Craig Moorhead.*

Drawing a deep breath, she rapped softly on the closed door.

"Who's there?" A deep but quiet voice called from inside.

"It's me, Eden."

A few silent moments ticked by before he called, "It's open."

Turning the knob, she pushed open the door and eased inside the small room. As the pressure-mounted door shut behind her, she hesitated to go very far into the room. She didn't want to encroach on his space; their relationship was strained enough. So, she stood there, waiting to be invited.

He was propped up on a stack of pillows in his bed, watching television. It was *Law & Order: SVU*, his favorite show. He turned his head, meeting her gaze. Raising his hand, he gestured her closer. "Come on over here where I can see you."

She did as he asked.

He observed her for a few moments. "You're looking well."

"Thank you. How are you feeling, Craig?"

"I'm all right, for a young fellow." A dry cough followed his words. "What brings you by?"

"I...just wanted to make sure you were okay and have a little talk with you. That is if you feel up to it."

He nodded, then indicated the upholstered wooden armchair next to his bed. "Sure. Sit on down."

She sat, resting her purse on her lap. "I've been doing a lot of thinking lately."

He chuckled. "Sounds like you."

She smiled in spite of her nerves, knowing this was his way. He always cracked jokes to break the tension, and when it came to the two of them, tension made up a large portion of their relationship. She'd come here today in hopes of changing that. "Anyway, I wanted to let you know that I've…forgiven you."

He frowned. "What you say?"

"I said, I've forgiven you. It took me a long time to… accept the reality of what happened between you and my mother, and how it's affected me." She knew the root of her mistrust for men lay in her childhood when she'd longed for the presence of a father. "I'm just ready to let go of all that negative energy. It's too great a burden."

His frown softening, he said, "I'm glad you came here to say that to me. But… I don't know if I'll ever be able to forgive myself."

She could hear the sadness in her voice. "Talk to me, Craig. Say what's in your heart."

He shifted a bit in bed, angling his body toward her. "I loved your mama. I swear I did. Even though I was fifteen years older than her, I loved her hard. Still do." A tear came to his eye, and he let it fall. "I was married, but the fire between me and Shirley had gone out years before. Jacinda was a ray of sunshine in my life." He smiled, a faraway look in his eyes. "I'd always see her there, working at the desk when I went down to the law library to study. Between the stress of law school and the demands of my wife and son… I needed somebody, you know? And she was there for me. Never meant for… things to turn out the way they did."

She nodded, reaching for his hand. "I know you didn't."

"That day you came here to tell me she was gone…" More tears filled his eyes. "Worse day of my life. I left her behind to try to work on my marriage, but soon as I got sick, Shirley and Craig Jr. just…left me here. Ain't seen or heard from either of 'em in years now." He raised his aged hands, brushing away the tears. "I know… I just know that if Jacinda was still living…"

"She'd be taking care of you." She squeezed his hands. "Mama never had anything bad to say about you, at least not to me. She always said you made the choice you thought was right, and I shouldn't fault you. Still, I held on to that anger for a long time."

"I don't blame you. Every little girl deserves to have her daddy around for her raising."

"That's true. But as I've gotten older, I've come to understand how complicated life and relationships can be. You just weren't there yet."

"I…don't even know how to apologize to you, Eden." He cast his eyes downward, as if ashamed of his choices. "What can I say that's going to make up for what I did?"

"You don't have to say anything." She smiled. "My mama loved you. And I love you, too, in my own odd little way. You did help bring me into this crazy and wonderful world."

He cried full-on then. Between sobs, he said, "You're a special girl. I'm honored to call you my daughter."

She brushed away her own tears. "And I'll be honored to call you Daddy." She stood, hugged his thin shoulders while he held her close. When she sat down again, she said, "I want you to know, I'm going to keep paying for your care, as long as you need it. Don't worry about Shirley and Craig Jr. As long as I'm around, you've got family."

He nodded. "Thank you, Eden. Thank you...for being so kindhearted. You're just like Jacinda... I know she'd be proud."

A vision of her mother's smiling face entered her mind.

I think he's right. Mama would be proud.

When Blaine got off the plane at LaGuardia Wednesday morning, he felt the buzz of excitement rolling through his body. Dressed in his best dark suit and wingtips, with his hair pulled back in a low ponytail, he was ready to take on the meeting at hand. He pulled his single small suitcase, his only luggage, along behind him as he headed for the baggage claim area to meet his private car service.

The black sedan navigated through the streets of New York, the driver maneuvering through the thick weekday traffic. Arriving in Manhattan at the Hamilton House headquarters, he exited the car and tipped the driver before heading upstairs to the thirtieth floor.

Tucking the suitcase away with the receptionist, he strode into the conference room. Rupert and Marvin were waiting there for him, seated toward the far end of the table.

Both men stood, and the three of them exchanged handshakes and greetings. Finally, with the small talk put aside, they all sat down. Rupert occupied the head of the table, with Marvin to his right and Blaine to his left.

Marvin smiled, lacing his fingers in front of him. "So, we're glad to see you back in New York, but I'm a bit surprised you asked to meet with us in person, Blaine."

"Yes," Rupert added, looking as constipated as ever. "You could have just faxed or mailed the contracts back to us. No need to hand-deliver them, you know."

Blaine smiled. "Oh, yes, gentlemen. I agree. Had I simply been returning contracts, I wouldn't be sitting here today." He rubbed his hands together. "I'll be taking an afternoon flight back to Atlanta, so let's get this meeting under way, shall we?"

"Certainly." Rupert's eyes narrowed slightly as if he wondered what Blaine had planned. Marvin looked similarly confused. Blaine relished their utter ignorance of what he was about to do for a few moments, then stood once again. He wanted to be able to look down on them while he said what he had to say. "When I first got the documents from you, I spent a good amount of time reading them, going over the terms, etcetera. My first impression was that it was a pretty standard change agreement, one that you'd simply altered a bit to fit our particular situation."

Rupert nodded. "That's exactly right. Very astute, Blaine."

He noted the condescension in Rupert's tone, but ignored it. He'd be singing a different tune soon enough. "Anyway, I took the document to Naiya and Eden for discussion and signing. And I've gotta tell you, neither of them was on board."

Marvin frowned. "No? So how did you proceed from there?"

"I didn't. Both of them walked out of the meeting, leaving the documents unsigned on the table."

Rupert scratched his chin. "Oh, I see. So, you've come here to brainstorm with us and work out some ways to get them to change their minds."

"So…how shall we start?" Marvin interjected. "I don't think we should go straight to threats of dropping Naiya from the label—that's a bit harsh. We'll need to use a light touch with them if we want them to agree to the terms."

"I agree. Perhaps a fruit basket or something nice from the corporate gift catalog would soften the tension a bit."

After watching them go back and forth for a while, Blaine could no longer contain his laugh. He laughed, loud and long.

Both men looked at him, their bewilderment obvious.

Marvin said, "Blaine, what's so funny? Have you gone off the deep end?"

He stifled his laughter, sobering up. "No, I haven't. Actually, I've got more clarity now than I've ever had."

"I see. So, you know how to proceed with this situation, then?" Rupert leaned forward in his seat as if anticipating his answer.

"Absolutely." He leaned forward as well, wanting to make sure they heard what he had to say. "I'm going to proceed by telling you that you can feel free to drop Against the Grain from your roster of labels."

Marvin recoiled. "Blaine, surely you don't mean that. Have you really thought this through?"

"Marvin's right. Have you considered how long your label will survive without our backing?" Rupert tugged his lapels. "It's a cruel world out there when you're a little fish in a big pond."

Marvin folded his arms over his chest, nodding in agreement.

Blaine scoffed. "I'm not as small a fish as you two might think. Not anymore."

"You aren't serious." Rupert's expression took on a hard set.

"I'm very serious." Blaine felt his jaw tighten and his resolve grow. "Let me tell you something. I believe in Naiya. I believe in her talent and in her vision. I also believe that Eden has been true to that vision. If following through with the album in its current iteration is a deal-breaker for you, so be it. I'm not going to sit by and let you destroy what we worked so hard on, in the name of some corporate focus-group bullshit."

Rupert's face folded into a grimace. "Blaine! I've never known you to be so unprofessional. I'm shocked, frankly."

"I'd rather be unprofessional than be a doormat. And as far as funding for my 'little label,' don't sweat it, boys. Because effective immediately, Against the Grain is a subsidiary of 404 Sound Recordings. And 404 will be funding her debut album. And just in case it should come up in one of your meetings, 404 Sound Recordings *is not* for sale." He shook his head, a triumphant smile on his face. "Now if you'll excuse me, I've got things to do. But feel free to kiss my 'unprofessional' ass as I leave." With one last look at their flabbergasted faces, he strode out.

By the time he climbed into the black sedan idling at the curb, he could no longer contain his elation. *I'm free! Now I can run my label the way I see fit.* And he knew exactly who he wanted to be the first to hear the great news.

Taking his phone out of his breast pocket, he dialed a number. "Hello, Naiya? I'm sure you're still upset with me, but I promise, what I'm about to say will make up for it."

After hearing Naiya's happy squeals and agreeing to meet with her at the studio next week to talk marketing strategy, he ended the call and dialed Eden. "Baby, guess what I just did?" He gave her a brief recap of the meeting.

"Wow, Blaine. That was incredibly bold. I'm proud of you."

"How proud?" He didn't bother to hide the teasing in his tone.

She gave as good as she got, as always. "Why don't you get your ass on that plane home, come over to my place and I'll show you."

Cupping his hand over the receiver, he said, "Driver, do you know a quicker way to LaGuardia?"

The driver chuckled. "Sure thing, chief."

Removing his hand from the mic, he said, "My flight lands at two. Why don't you meet me at the airport?"

"I'll be there, honey."

He licked his lips, already anticipating her very special brand of welcome.

I can't wait to get home.

Hours later, they were kissing their way into his bedroom, barely able to keep their hands off each other. Fumbling around for the light switch while reaching over her shoulder, he finally gave up, depending on his other senses to guide them toward his bed while he kissed her.

Pulling back from her sweet lips, he asked, "Is there a reason you chose this dress to pick me up from the airport in?"

She looked down at the fitted black minidress, feigning innocence. "What, this? I just threw it on so you wouldn't be waiting long."

He chuckled. "You lie so well I almost believe it." He punctuated his words with more kisses as his hands circled the bare skin of her thighs, just below the hem of the dress.

"Mmm." She moaned into his ear. "Why don't you let me congratulate you...my way?" She grasped his arms, turning him so his back was to the bed.

"What do you have in mind?" Moments later, as she stripped him of his clothes, pushed him down to sit on the bed, and knelt before him, her intentions became clear. He growled as her lips closed over his hard shaft, weaving his fingers through her hair. "Shit."

She hummed, the vibration adding to the pleasure of

her warm, wet mouth wrapped around him. Her head moved back and forth in time with her impassioned sucking, and he felt his whole body start to tremble. Letting his hands slip down to her shoulders, he gently pushed her away. "If you keep that up I'm gonna…"

"Come?" She teased the tip with her tongue. "What if that's what I want?"

He jerked in response. "No, baby. I want to be inside you when it happens." He helped her up off the floor, drawing her onto his bed. She knelt over him, raising her arms as he snatched off her dress. The red lace bra and thong set she wore beneath only increased the fire in his blood.

"Grab a condom from my nightstand, baby," he instructed softly.

She did as he asked, and to his surprise, rolled the protection down over his shaft.

Unable to wait another moment to be inside her, he nudged her into place. Crooking his finger, he slid her panties to one side, then guided her down onto his dick.

He gritted his teeth against the blinding pleasure as she began to ride, rolling her hips as she held on to his waist. She moved her hands up, splaying them across his abdomen as she shifted forward, circling her hips like she was working an imaginary hula hoop.

It wasn't long before he heard her moans climbing higher, indicating an oncoming orgasm. He grabbed her waist and thrust up, letting his hips piston to meet hers. She tossed her head back and screamed his name while her body pulsated around him. Moments later, his own orgasm raced through his body, the force of it making him growl and shake.

In the aftermath, they lay sprawled across his comforter. Holding her in his arms felt like second nature, like destiny. He crooked his finger beneath her chin, guiding her face until she looked into his eyes.

"What is it, Blaine?"

"Stay with me, Eden." He was too far gone to worry about whether he sounded weak. He needed her, and there was no way around it. "Forever."

She offered him a soft smile. "I'll think about it."

He chuckled. "C'mon, baby. Don't tease a brotha. Not at a moment like this."

She shook her head. "Don't worry. I'll stay." She snuggled closer to him.

And as he held her body close to his, he felt a sense of peace like nothing he'd ever experienced before.

Epilogue

January

Raising the steaming cup of cocoa to her lips, Eden stood by the large bay window, watching the swirling snow outside. The picturesque image of the fluffy white flakes floating over the peaks of the Loveland Ski Resort provided the perfect backdrop for their honeymoon. She took a long sip, savoring the chocolaty warmth of the beverage and the warmth she felt inside.

Blaine walked up behind her, wearing nothing but a pair of silk boxers. He draped his strong arms around her waist. Feeling the hard lines of his body pressed against her made her shiver, but not from the cold. "Hey, you. What are you thinking about?"

"About how lucky I am. How happy I am to be your wife." She set the cocoa down on the windowsill and turned within the circle of his arms.

"Funny. I was thinking about how glad I am we chose to marry this way…just the two of us, the justice of the peace and the mountain."

She smiled at the memory of the previous day's mountaintop ceremony. As local Justice Sophia Llewellyn presided, they'd said their vows surrounded by the azure sky, the puffy white clouds and the chilly Colorado winds. He'd worn a charcoal wool suit, and she'd worn a fully lined formal white pantsuit and matching hat, accented with faux fur and Swarovski crystals. Instead of carrying a bouquet, she'd worn a crystal-studded faux-fur muff. "It was a wonderful day."

"A wonderful night, too, if I recall." He brushed his lips over the hollow of her throat.

She blushed, remembering how he'd carried her over the threshold of their cozy little mountainside cabin, slowly undressed her and made passionate love to her until she'd cried tears of joy into his strong shoulder. "You'll get no complaints from me."

He leaned in then and kissed her softly. "I can't believe it took me so many years to get out of my own way and do right by you."

"Me, either." She grinned, touched his cheek. "But better late than never, as they say."

"I love you, Eden Voss Woodson."

With the happy tears gathering in her eyes once again, she whispered, "I love you, too."

He pulled her in for his kiss, and before long, he carried her to the bed again.

And as the moon ascended over the Colorado mountains, her cries of ecstasy rose on the cold night air.

* * * * *

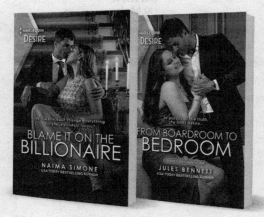

"Come here," he said, his voice suddenly hard. "I want to show
you something."

There was a big white tent that was still closed, reserved for
an evening hors d'oeuvre session for people who had bought
premium tickets, and he compelled her inside. It was already set
up with tables and tablecloths, everything elegant and dainty,
and exceedingly Maxfield. Though there were bottles of Cowboy
Wines on each table, along with bottles of Maxfield select.

But they were not apparently here to look at the wine, or indeed
anything else that was set up. Which she discovered when he
cupped her chin with firm fingers and looked directly into her eyes.

"I've done nothing but think about you for two weeks. I want
you. Not just something hot and quick against a wall. I need you
in a bed, Wren. We need some time to explore this. To explore
each other."

She blinked. She had not expected that.

He'd been avoiding her and she'd been so sure it was because
he didn't want this.

But he was here in a suit.

And he had a look of intent gleaming in those green eyes.

She realized then she'd gotten it all wrong.

"I...I agree."

She also hadn't expected to agree.

"I want you now," she whispered, and before she could stop herself, she was up on her tiptoes and kissing that infuriating mouth.

She wanted to sigh with relief. She had been so angry at him. So angry at the way he had ignored this. Because how dare he? He had never ignored the anger between them. No. He had taken every opportunity to goad and prod her in anger. So why, why had he ignored this?

But he hadn't.

They were devouring each other, and neither of them cared that there were people outside. His large hands palmed her ass, pulling her up against his body so she could feel just how hard he was for her. She arched against him, gasping when the center of her need came into contact with his rampant masculinity.

She didn't understand the feelings she had for this man. Where everything about him that she found so disturbing was also the very thing that drove her into his arms.

Too big. Too rough. Crass. Untamable. He was everything she detested, everything she desired.

All that, and he was distracting her from an event that she had planned. Which was a cardinal sin in her book. And she didn't even care.

He set her away from him suddenly, breaking their kiss. "Not now," he said, his voice rough. "Tonight. All night. You. In my bed."

Don't miss what happens next in...
Claiming the Rancher's Heir
by New York Times *bestselling author Maisey Yates!*

Available November 2020 wherever
Harlequin Desire books and ebooks are sold.

Harlequin.com